Liars
and
Fools

Liars
and
Fools

ROBIN STEVENSON

ORCA BOOK PUBLISHERS

Library and Archives Canada Cataloguing in Publication

Stevenson, Robin, 1968-
Liars and fools / written by Robin Stevenson.

Issued also in an electronic format.
ISBN 978-1-55469-248-4

I. Title.
PS8637.T487L52 2010   jC813'.6   C2010-903573-9

First published in the United States, 2010
Library of Congress Control Number: 2010929088

Summary: Still grieving the loss of her mother, Fiona resists the idea of
moving on with her life, especially when her father starts dating a psychic.

Mixed Sources
Product group from well-managed forests,
controlled sources and recycled wood or fiber
www.fsc.org Cert no. SW-COC-000952
© 1996 Forest Stewardship Council

*Orca Book Publishers is dedicated to preserving the environment and has printed this book
on paper certified by the Forest Stewardship Council.*

Orca Book Publishers gratefully acknowledges the support for its publishing
programs provided by the following agencies: the Government of Canada through the
Canada Book Fund and the Canada Council for the Arts, and the Province of British
Columbia through the BC Arts Council and the Book Publishing Tax Credit.

Cover Design by Teresa Bubela
Cover photo by Getty Images
Typesetting by Jasmine Devonshire
Author photo by David Lowes

ORCA BOOK PUBLISHERS
PO Box 5626, STN. B
VICTORIA, BC CANADA
V8R 6S4

ORCA BOOK PUBLISHERS
PO Box 468
CUSTER, WA USA
98240-0468

www.orcabook.com
Printed and bound in Canada.

13 12 11 10 • 4 3 2 1

To David and Genevieve

one

"Grand Opening!" Abby read out loud. "Free Psychic Readings! Today Only!"

She was pointing at a hand-lettered sign in front of a small store called *The Mystic Heart Healing Center and Gift Shop*. I stepped closer and peered through the window. Inside, brightly colored scarves billowed like clouds from a high ceiling. "Looks like one of those incense and wind chime places," I said, wrinkling my nose.

"Want to go in?"

"About as much as I want to get my math test back on Monday. Come on, let's go get ice cream."

"Oh, it'll be fun." Abby pulled me toward the door, laughing. "Maybe your psychic reading will tell you whether you passed."

"Like I need a psychic for that." I reluctantly followed her into the store, and my shoulder brushed against a cluster of dangling bamboo pipes, setting off a melodic jangle. "See?" I muttered. "Wind chimes. Told you."

The shop was tiny but crammed to overflowing with candles, Buddha statues, carved elephants, Tarot cards, crystals, beads, aromatherapy jars and books. One title caught my eye: *How to Read Palms and Predict the Future.* I turned away quickly, trying to stop my thoughts from rushing toward the whirlpool that was always lurking at the back of my mind, threatening to pull me in. So many little things could make me think of my mother. So many thoughts were best avoided.

"Too much incense," I said, clearing my throat. "Makes my eyes water."

"I like the smell," Abby said. "What is it, lavender? Or lilac? Oh hey, look." She gestured to the back of the store, where a small table was set up. A woman with wild red curls and big silver hoop earrings was standing there, fussing over the precise arrangement of the floral tablecloth. "She must be the psychic. Come on, Fiona."

"You go ahead," I said.

The woman looked up. "Welcome to the Mystic Heart. I'm Penny."

"Can we get free psychic readings? Like the sign says?" Abby asked.

The woman laughed. "Not from me, I'm afraid. My friend Kathy is giving free readings, but she just nipped across the street to get a coffee."

"Let's go," I said to Abby. "It could be ages."

The door opened, and the wind chimes jangled again as a tall woman in black cords and a thick sweater came in, gripping a large paper coffee cup in each hand. She grinned at us. "You girls waiting for me?"

"If you're going to tell us the future, we are." Abby grinned back. "You don't look like a psychic though. We thought she was the psychic." She nodded toward the red-haired store owner.

The woman laughed. "Nope, Penny's the hard-headed business owner, and I'm the psychic." She let the door swing closed behind her and handed one of the coffees to the red-headed woman. "I guess I don't look the part, do I?"

A picture flashed into my mind: the palm reader Mom and I saw the fall I was starting grade six. We'd been at a fair—roller coasters, candy floss, Ferris wheels, all that stuff—and there had been a tent set up with a sign out front that read: *Psychic readings! Palmistry! Tarot!*

Mom had pointed and giggled. *Want to do it?*
Nah. Let's go on the Scrambler.

She made a face. *Not right after lunch. Actually, not ever. Come on. It'll be good for a laugh.*

Inside the tent, an old woman introduced herself as Joanna. She had pale skin as softly wrinkled as tissue paper, red lipstick smudged onto her front teeth, dangling silver earrings and a sparkly purple scarf draped over her shoulders.

She took my hand in hers and told me that I was good at art and had a creative mind, and that I was determined and strong-willed. Then she took Mom's hand and studied it for a few seconds. *You're a lot like your daughter,* she said solemnly. *Creative, strong-willed, adventurous.* Mom winked at me, and I tried not to giggle.

I see many, many grandchildren, the woman continued. *Yes, you will have many grandchildren.*

I started to laugh. Not if it was up to me, she wouldn't.

Mom nudged me with her knee under the table. *And how about traveling? Do you see any traveling? On a boat, maybe?*

Yes, yes. You will still be traveling when you are an old woman. And you have a very long life line. She traced a line on my mother's palm with a long red finger nail. *Yes, yes. A very long life line.*

Well, that's good to know, Mom said, laughing.

Six months later, she was dead.

"Earth to Fiona," Abby said, nudging me hard.

"What?" I blinked.

She looked exasperated. "Haven't you been listening at all? She wants you to go first."

"Me?" I looked over at the psychic, who was sipping her coffee and watching me over the rim of the paper cup. Her sweater was blue with white snowflakes, and her dark hair was tied back in a loose ponytail.

"I just have a feeling about this," she said.

I resisted the urge to roll my eyes. "I don't want a reading, thanks. Abby's the one who wanted to come in."

"I know it sounds weird, but…" The woman hesitated. "I feel as if there is someone who has a message for you. I don't mean to pry, but have you lost someone close to you?"

Abby—who usually prides herself on being the Voice of Logic—looked at me wide-eyed. "Fiona! That's…"

I cut her off. "Fine," I said. "I'll go first."

The psychic adjusted two chairs so they were facing each other and motioned me to sit down with her. I hung back for a second, suddenly nervous. "So how does this work?"

She laughed again. She had a nice laugh: low and easy. "No crystal balls or tea leaves, I'm afraid. I'm rather boring. Just sit quietly for a minute and I'll see what I pick up."

"Do I close my eyes?"

"Only if you want to."

I sat down, stared at my sneakers and tried to relax. I didn't believe this stuff for a second, but this woman seemed nice enough, and I didn't want to be rude. At least she wasn't as weird as that awful palm reader.

"I see waves," the woman said slowly. She closed her eyes.

I caught my breath and looked up at her. "Like in an ocean?"

"Maybe...I think so. Yes, it is an ocean," she said. "I can smell salt and hear the waves crashing. It's dark..."

I couldn't breathe. I couldn't take my eyes off her face.

She opened her eyes and looked at me. "You're awfully pale. Do you want me to stop?"

I shook my head. "Keep going."

Frowning, she closed her eyes for a few seconds. When she looked at me again, her expression was puzzled. "I see bright lights," she said. "Dazzling. Fireworks, perhaps."

Flares. Red and white parachute flares, burning bright a thousand feet above the waves...

"And I'm picking up strong emotions. Fear. Intense fear. And regret." She leaned toward me. "Does this make any sense to you?"

"Yeah." I blinked away tears and tasted salt. "Yeah, it does."

"Someone...a woman, I think? Older than you?"

"My mother."

"Yes. She wants you to know that she loves you"— the woman paused as if she was listening to something I couldn't hear—"and that she is sorry. She wants you to know that she is sorry."

My eyes were stinging, and I couldn't hold back the tears any longer. I took a long choking breath and rubbed my sleeve across my eyes. "Can you see her?"

"It's fading out now. Just darkness."

"Is that it then?"

"I'm afraid so. I'm not getting anything else. Are you all right? I know how overwhelming this can be."

"I'm fine." I forced a smile.

"It's hard to know how to interpret things sometimes. It could be the past or the future. The waves might not even be real waves at all. They could be symbolic." She sounded worried. Apparently my smile hadn't fooled her.

I stood up and put my hand on the chair back for balance. I felt shaky. "They were real waves."

Abby was watching me and biting her bottom lip. "Are you okay?"

"Fine." I zipped my jacket up and shoved my hands into my pockets. "Can we please go now?"

"You sure you don't want to stay for a few minutes?" the woman asked. "You still look sort of pale." The wind chimes jangled again, and a cluster of middle-aged women wandered in, talking and laughing loudly. "Oh dear. Looks like I have some more clients." She looked at Abby. "You're next though, if you'd like a reading too."

I jumped in. "Abby, I want to go. You can stay if you want, but I'm going."

Abby cast a longing glance at the psychic. "Maybe some other time," she said. "I'd better go with my friend."

The woman rummaged in her purse and pulled something out. "My card. In case you want another reading. Or if you need to talk about this one."

"Thanks." I took the card and put it in my jeans pocket without looking at it. I could almost see the waves crashing on the reef and the flares lighting up the darkness. I could feel my mother's fear, tight and urgent beneath my ribs.

As soon as we were outside, I turned to Abby and held up my hand. "I don't want to talk about it, okay?" I started to walk quickly down the sidewalk, the late afternoon air cool and damp against my face.

"Come on, Fiona." Abby hurried to keep up. "You look totally freaked out."

"I'm not," I protested. Actually, I was, but I also felt closer to my mother than I had in months and I didn't want to ruin it by talking about what had just happened.

"Fiona? Don't get carried away here. I know I got excited back there when she said she had a message for you, but let's face it: the things she said were pretty vague."

"Vague?" I stared at her. "An ocean? Flares?"

"She didn't say that. She just said waves. You were the one who said ocean."

I frowned, trying to remember.

"Waves could be a standard opening line, you know? Someone else might not say anything, or they might look puzzled, and then she'd throw out another word. Trees or a road or whatever."

I wrapped my arms about myself tightly and tried not to listen.

"Look, you can't take it seriously," Abby said. "She was pretty good at her routine, but it's just acting and guesswork."

"You were the one who wanted to go in there."

"Yeah, for a laugh. Not because I believe in it. There is no way anyone can really bring messages from people who have died. You know that, right?"

"I don't want to talk about it, okay?"

Abby was quiet for a minute, walking along by my side, looking unhappy. "So. Ice cream?" she said at last.

Ice cream was the reason we had come downtown. There's this place at the mall that will mix any kind of topping right into whatever flavor ice cream you want. Mom used to get cherries and Oreo cookies in vanilla ice cream, but Abby and I always got gummy bears. "Yeah," I said, trying to smile at her. "Ice cream."

But I had a feeling that even gummy bears in chocolate ice cream weren't going to make me feel better today.

two

I was still thinking about the psychic woman on Monday morning as I crouched low over the handlebars of my bicycle, eyes watering and fingers half-frozen in my thin gloves. Gravel skidded under my tires as I coasted down the hill and into the boatyard. Across the parking lot, a forest of masts rose from the water. The sky was a hard cold blue, the sun a flat white disc. I jumped off my bike and leaned it against the chain-link fence. A stiff breeze blew steadily onto shore. I hugged myself and shivered. It had officially been spring for a week, but the air still held the damp chill of winter.

It wasn't quite eight, but already there were a few people around, working on their boats, carrying gear along the narrow docks, drinking coffee from travel mugs. I ignored them and they ignored me.

I figured that everyone knew what had happened to Mom. I'd even overheard two women talking about her in the marina washroom once, gossiping while they washed their hands and fixed their hair.

Jennifer wrote her own ticket, one of them said. *Not that I'm saying she had it coming, but there's gutsy and then there's stupid.* Through the crack in the stall door I could see the backs of their heads, one blond and one gray. Mother and daughter, maybe. For a moment I thought about bursting out and shouting at them, and making them feel terrible. But underneath my anger was something like shame. Dad had known Mom was taking too many risks. He'd tried to get her to take safety precautions. And what had I done? I'd taken my mother's side.

So I didn't shout at the women. I stayed hidden in the stall, my cheeks burning, until they left.

Everyone down here at the marina stayed away from me now. It was like that at school too. Except for Abby, people seemed to avoid me. Maybe they thought disaster was contagious. Or maybe they didn't know what to say.

The tide was low, and the ramp down to the docks was steep and wet from the morning dew. I walked quickly, almost running, my feet finding the nonskid strips on the steel walkway. School started at 8:45, so I only had a few minutes. I would have liked to have more time, but Dad would wonder why I was leaving for school so early. He didn't know I still came here. At least, I didn't think he knew. We didn't talk about it.

As always, setting foot on the docks calmed me down. I didn't really understand it, but whenever I was around the boats, it was as if something changed inside me: slowed down, settled. Softened and lifted me up. It felt like magic of some kind. It was the one place I could still see my mother's face clearly when I closed my eyes. The one place that I could think about her without getting sucked into the whirlpool of memory and guilt.

Which was why I had to keep coming, no matter what my dad said.

And if the psychic was right, if my mother was out there somewhere, thinking about me, then where was she more likely to be than here?

Our boat, *Eliza J*, was at the end of E-dock. I could see her sitting there, heavy and solid in the water, her white hull stained with greenish streaks, the blue canvas of her dodger and sail cover faded from the sun. I wished I could spend the day scrubbing her deck and polishing the surface rust from her stainless steel stanchions and rails. I looked around to make sure no one was paying any attention to me; then I stepped on board. The boat rocked slightly under my weight.

The cockpit floor was dirty, and thick green algae grew in rings of slime where water pooled around the drains. The companionway boards were locked in place. They'd been locked in place for a year: the padlock was probably rusted shut by now. I pressed my nose against a porthole, trying to get a glimpse of the dark cabin down below. I could see the table folded against the wall, and the edge of the portside berth. My berth, the one I used to sleep on. I remembered the scratchy-soft feel of the beige fabric against my cheek and the faint smell of it: mildew mixed with the citrus tang of laundry soap and something else, something almost sweet.

"Hi, Mom," I whispered. That was all I ever said. I didn't try to have conversations with her or anything; I'm not crazy. It was just that I could remember her most vividly here. I could picture her standing at the tiller, laughing as *Eliza J* sailed into the wind, adjusting the sails, talking to me. *Fiona, tighten up that jib sheet, would you? Isn't this absolutely gorgeous sailing? Be a love and grab those cookies from down below. I'm starving.*

There was a sharp stabbing feeling in my throat, and my eyes were suddenly wet. It was a relief to feel something. Lately it felt as if even my memories of my mom were slipping away. No one talked about her anymore. Not Dad, not my Aunt Joni, not Tom.

It seemed like they were all starting to forget her.
I wouldn't let that happen. Not ever.

I pedaled hard, flew down the streets to school and
managed to slip into my seat seconds before the bell
rang. Just as well. I'd been late way too many times this
year. For the first few months after the accident, the
teachers all treated me like I was made of glass. They
gave me tentative smiles, asked if I was okay, told me
they were there if I wanted to talk—that kind of thing.
Even if I was late or skipped homework, they never
gave me a hard time about it.

Lately though, it seemed like there was some kind
of time limit on grieving. The first anniversary of
Mom's death was March 1, which was three weeks ago.
Maybe they had it on their calendars. Maybe they'd
talked about me at a staff meeting and agreed that it
was time I got my act together. All I knew for sure was
that the sympathetic nods had recently been replaced
with lunch-hour detentions. My free pass had expired.

I looked around the room, only half-listening
to the announcements over the PA system. Abby
was grinning at me from the next row. I grinned
back, but stopped smiling abruptly when I saw what
Mrs. Moskin was handing out. Last week's math quiz.

Ugh. The teacher gave me a funny look when she put my paper on my desk: almost a smile, but not quite. So maybe I'd done okay?

I lifted the corner and peeked at the grade. Nope, not okay. Not even close to okay. A fail. Dad was going to flip. For a moment, I considered dropping the paper in the garbage and not telling him, but I'd be bringing a report card home in a month. He'd find out anyway. After last term's grades, it wouldn't exactly come as a shock.

I folded the paper in half and started to stick it in my binder. The back of my math test was covered with scribbles and notes. I paused and ran a finger along the first line. It read: *20° 52.45' N; 156° 40.77' W. Lahaina Harbor, Maui.*

I'd been daydreaming, imagining sailing to Hawaii. It was a trip Mom and I had planned to do together someday. Dad used to say he'd meet us there: he got too seasick to want to spend much time offshore. I picked up my pen and drew a little sailboat on the edge of the page, its sails set for a downwind course across 2,300 nautical miles of blue-green ocean. I closed my eyes for a moment. Dolphins, sunsets, Pacific Ocean trade winds…

Mrs. Moskin cleared her throat.

"Would you care to join us, Fiona?"

My cheeks flushed hot. "Sorry?"

Mrs. Moskin fluffed her hair. She's always doing that. She's a small, skinny woman with thin white hair and a pink scalp that shows through in places. Her eyebrows are penciled on, two brown lines arching above pale blue eyes. She's twitchy, and everyone calls her the Mouse. Though not to her face, of course.

"Unless you have something more important you'd rather be doing?" she asked me.

"Well…"

The Mouse read my mind. "It was a rhetorical question. I think I'd rather you didn't answer it." She took her beady eyes off me and addressed the class. "As you'll know if you were paying attention, I was talking about the science fair," she said. "This will be a chance to explore any topic that interests you. You can pose any question you want, provided you can come up with a hypothesis and devise an experiment to put it to the test."

"Can we do our project with a partner?" I asked.

Mrs. Moskin nodded. "Yes." She looked at me and then at Abby. "If you do your project with a partner, you will share the grade. So be sure you pair up with someone who will do their share of the work."

As if I'd ever let Abby down. I glanced across the aisle, trying to catch her eye, but she quickly looked down at her desk. My stomach started to hurt.

Ayla Neilson put up her hand. "Mrs. Moskin?"

"Yes, Ayla." Mrs. Moskin sounded tired. Whoever said there is no such thing as a stupid question had never met Ayla.

Ayla twisted a red-blond curl around her finger. "Well, what kind of topic? Like, what is a science topic? Do we have to dissect anything? Because I don't believe in killing animals or, like, plants or anything."

The Mouse sat down on the edge of her desk. "Any topic, as I said, can be suitable for scientific exploration. You do not have to dissect anything. I don't usually feel a need to spell this out, but let me be clear: please do not kill anything. If you have a topic in mind and have questions about it, please see me after class."

I looked over at Abby again, but she didn't look up. "*Pssst*. Abby."

Mrs. Moskin frowned at me. "Fiona. Please save your private conversations for lunch hour."

As the morning went on, I felt worse and worse. I couldn't believe Abby would actually think I wouldn't do my share of the work. We'd done practically every project together since we started hanging out in the fourth grade. We were always partners. Always.

By the time the lunch bell finally rang, I wanted to go home. I dragged my feet to the cafeteria and sat down beside Abby in my usual spot. Mrs. Moskin's words were stuck in my head, and I couldn't decide whether to bring up the subject or not. I crumpled my paper lunch bag in my fist and sighed. I didn't think I could stand to hear Abby admit she didn't want to work with me.

Beside me, Abby pulled out a set of matching plastic containers. She took the lids off and stacked them neatly, uncovering a sandwich, some applesauce, and sliced carrots and celery. She brought the same thing every day. "How did you do on the math test?" she asked.

I wondered if my answer was going to make a difference to whether she'd want to work with me. "Not too well."

Abby waited, eyebrows raised.

"Okay, okay. It was bad. A fail." I really wanted to ask her about being partners for the science project, but I was scared to push for an answer. As long as we didn't talk about it, I wouldn't have to hear her say no.

"Can I see?"

I pulled the page out of my binder and held it out to her. Abby took it, biting her lip when she saw the grade. "Fiona! I told you how to do these problems. They're exactly the same as the ones we studied." She turned the paper over and studied the scribbles on the back for a few minutes before handing it back to me.

"I don't understand how you can do this stuff but flunk an easy math test."

I didn't answer right away. I did okay in math last year, but after Mom died, I missed a lot of school—most of the last couple of months of sixth grade. Dad had stopped going to work. He stayed awake all night and slept on the couch in the afternoon. He didn't care if I went to school. I don't think he even noticed. There was never any food in the house unless Joni brought dinner over, and in the end I went to stay with her and Tom for a while. Eventually Dad got better, and I moved home and went back to school for grade seven, but I got a lot of bad stomach aches, and I had a hard time concentrating.

Anyway, somewhere in there the math itself had gotten weird. The Mouse started wanting us to add letters instead of numbers, and move triangles around on grids. "I hate math," I told Abby at last.

She pointed at the pages of equations on the back of my test. "What do you call this?"

I picked up the top page. Latitudes and longitudes. The course I'd been plotting from Victoria to Maui. Sailing west at an average speed of 5 knots...2,308 miles divided by 5...equals 461 hours...equals 19 days. Of course, the wind is unpredictable and 5 knots might be unrealistic. Still, it shouldn't take much more than 3 weeks.

I didn't know why I was wasting time thinking about the trip. It wasn't like it was ever going to happen, not without Mom. The numbers started to blur and I put the page down, blinking back tears. "That's not math," I said. "That's sailing."

three

Dad and I live near Willows Beach in a yellow stucco house with blue wooden trim and a wide front porch. It is only a few blocks from the water—close to the marina—and Dad always says that if we had to buy it now, we couldn't afford more than the downstairs bathroom. Mom and Dad moved here when they got married, and I've lived here my whole life. We've got tons of pictures all over the walls: Mom and Dad at their wedding; me as a toddler dolled up in dresses before I was old enough to object; the three of us at the beach or camping or on vacation in Tofino. Mom and Dad are holding hands in most of them, smiling at each other or at me. None of the pictures are from the last few years.

I pedaled slowly on my way home. Dad never got home before five thirty, and I hated being alone in the house. I usually went to Joni's after school, but she had called this morning to say she was sick and that I shouldn't come in case she was contagious. I'd asked Abby if I could go to her place, but she'd said she had a piano lesson.

I slowed to a stop before I turned onto my street. Maybe I'd go to the marina and hang out there for a while. Dad wouldn't know the difference. I could spend an hour on *Eliza J*, even clean the deck and the stanchions, if I could borrow a hose or find a few rags. I could be home by five, boil up some pasta or heat up some soup, have dinner ready by the time Dad got home. I sped up, dropped my bike in the driveway and ran into the too-quiet, too-empty house. I crammed a few rags and a water bottle into my backpack, got back on my bike and pedaled as fast as I could toward the marina.

*
· *
*. *

The wind had died down since the morning; the sun was warmer and the marina busier. A boat was making its way to the dock, its sails bundled loosely on the deck, an older man at the helm carefully maneuvering into a slip. Some people sat in their cockpits, talking loudly, laughing; others were striding down the docks, lugging coolers to their boats, untying lines, getting ready to go out.

I ignored them all, walking quickly past them to get to E-dock. The first job was to get rid of that green sludge around the cockpit drains, I decided. Mom had been a total clean freak when it came to the boat. In the house she sometimes let things slide, but the boat had to be perfect. Now *Eliza J* just sat there, her deck grimy, her steel railings rust-stained and her waterline dark green with algae. It made me sad to see it, but at the same time, I couldn't stay away. I'd feel like I was abandoning *Eliza J* if I didn't at least do what I could.

As I got closer, something caught my eye. A white and blue rectangle, dangling from her bow rail. I squinted.

FOR SALE.

It didn't make sense. I stared at the sign. It wasn't our phone number on it. *Blue Pacific Yachts*, it said. A yacht broker. I thought of *Eliza J* as Mom's boat, but legally, she was Dad's now. And Dad was selling her. I stood, staring at the sign for a long moment, barely able to breathe. He couldn't do this. He couldn't sell *Eliza J*.

"You okay, kid?" a man's voice asked.

I spun around. It was the old guy who owned the blue-hulled powerboat in the next slip. "Fine," I said. My voice didn't come out right; it sounded tinny and hollow, like it was echoing inside my skull.

He nodded. "Beautiful boat."

"Yes. She is." My eyes were suddenly stinging, and everything blurred. I turned and walked away, opening my eyes wide. If I blinked, the tears would spill out, and I was scared they might never stop.

Before Mom died, I hardly ever cried. Once when I was tying up *Eliza J*, a gust had pushed the boat away from the dock and the rope had torn a layer of skin from my palms. Some of our boat neighbors—including the old guy who had just spoken to me, as well as all the others who now nod to me and look away—made a huge fuss. Mom squeezed my shoulder. *Fiona never cries,* she said. She grinned at me. *Next time, let go of the rope.*

✦

I sat on the couch, half-watching TV while I waited for Dad to get home. With every minute that passed, my anger got hotter and harder and more solid inside me. I knew Mom wasn't coming back, but that didn't give Dad the right to get rid of the things that were most precious to her. All the things I wanted to say to him were rushing through my head, all the angry words crammed together in broken sentences and unfinished thoughts. He was going to be upset that I'd gone to the marina, but too bad. I couldn't believe he'd put Mom's boat up for sale without even telling me.

What if I'd gone down there one day and the boat was gone? My stomach was starting to hurt like it did right after Mom disappeared.

Finally I heard Dad's key in the lock. The front door opened and closed. I could hear him taking off his shoes and hanging up his coat.

"Hi there, Fiona. How was your day?" Dad walked through the living room and right past me without looking up. He started sifting through a pile of mail that the cleaner had left stacked on the kitchen counter.

I wanted to hit him or throw something across the room. "Not so good," I said.

"Uh-huh." He ripped open one envelope. "Bills, bills…"

He wasn't even pretending to listen. He obviously didn't care how my day was. "Why bother asking?" I said.

"Huh?" He looked up. "What's that?"

"Nothing." I turned off the TV, stood up and headed upstairs. I don't think Dad even noticed.

* * *

I was probably the only kid in my school who had no phone and no computer in her room. Mom had always said technology was bad for relationships.

Personally, I couldn't see how making communication more difficult was supposed to help my friendships. Anyway, Dad had both a computer and a phone in his own room now. It made enforcing Mom's rule with me seem a bit hypocritical.

Mom had been opposed to technology on boats too. She was a purist, she'd said. She'd believed in doing things the traditional way—roller-furling systems were for fat and lazy weekend sailors who couldn't be bothered to leave the comfort of their cockpits to adjust the sails; radar was just one more thing to break down; GPS navigation systems and other high-tech gadgets were bad, bad, bad. In her words, these things were destroying the closeness of the relationship between sailor and sea.

It was one of the things she and Dad used to fight about. *Bad enough that you take off to the South Pacific or the Caribbean for weeks at a time,* Dad had complained. I'd been sitting at the top of the stairs, crouched on the landing and straining to hear every word. *The least you can do is take along the technology to communicate. A satellite phone, maybe. Tell me, how would a satellite phone interfere with your experience?*

Peter, if you don't understand by now, there's not much point in me trying to explain. Mom's voice was angry and loud.

Well, one of those GPS *rescue things at least, so the coast guard could find you if you needed help. You don't even have to use the damn thing unless it's an emergency.*

Mom shrugged him off. *I'll be fine, Peter.*

Right. You'll be fine, Dad said. *And that's all you care about, isn't it? You, you, you.* He stood up. *I've had enough of this, Jennifer. It isn't fair to Fiona or to me.*

I leaned over the railing. *Leave me out of it, Dad,* I shouted. *Anyway, Mom knows what she's doing.*

Dad looked up, red-faced and angry. *Fiona! What are you doing up?*

Go back to bed, honey. Mom's voice was firm, but she smiled up at me, like she was glad I was on her side.

Stop trying to tell her what to do all the time, I said to Dad. *She knows what she's doing. You don't even know how to sail.*

He opened his mouth and closed it again, shaking his head as if he couldn't find the words. Then he turned and walked right out the front door. At eleven o'clock at night. Mom made hot chocolate for me and told me about the trip to the South Pacific she was planning. She was going to fly down and spend three weeks with a friend who had been cruising for the last two years. She showed me a picture of the boat: a new-looking, white thirty-six footer with a center-cockpit, flashy, but not as pretty as *Eliza J.*

I tried to sound like I was excited for her, but I couldn't help thinking about what I had overheard. They'd had arguments before, but this was different. What did Dad mean, *I've had enough of this*? For the first time, I wondered if they might actually get divorced.

When I was little, Mom had a different boat—a smaller one, called *Banana Split*. Dad used to come sailing occasionally, but he never liked it much. He got seasick, and anti-nausea drugs made him sleepy. And *Banana Split* was so small, he couldn't stand up in the cabin or stretch out in the bed. When I was eight, Mom sold *Banana Split* and bought *Eliza J*. Bigger beds, standing headroom, and sturdy enough for any conditions. She wanted to do a long trip: the three of us, sailing down to Mexico or across the Pacific to Hawaii, living on the boat together for months or years.

But Dad wouldn't do it. He said that even on the new boat, he would still get seasick, and besides, he couldn't afford to take that kind of time off work. Mom was—in her own words—devastated. They started fighting all the time. And Dad stopped sailing completely. He wouldn't even set foot on *Eliza J*.

Mom got more and more into it and started crewing on other people's boats, helping them on long passages in the South Pacific and the Caribbean. She took off for weeks at a time. You'd think Dad would have been happy that she'd found a way to pursue her dreams, but all he said was that it cost way too much money. He was always going on about what things cost.

I hated it when my parents fought, but I was secretly glad I didn't have to share sailing with my dad. It was the one time my mom slowed down enough to really talk to me. It was our special thing.

*   *   *

Now I sat on the edge of Dad's bed, on the side that used to be my mom's. Back when she was alive, there were always messy stacks of books and magazines on her bedside table. A few weeks after she died, Dad tidied it up. It stayed bare for months, but slowly he had taken over Mom's side, so now he had two bedside tables covered with his junk. I didn't like to look at it. It was like even the space Mom used to occupy was slowly disappearing.

I looked at the phone and considered calling Abby. Then I remembered the way she'd looked away from me when Mrs. Moskin said we could work with partners for the science project. I still hadn't asked her about it, and she hadn't brought it up either.

Maybe I should call that psychic instead. I wondered how much it would cost to see her again. Probably Abby was right, and psychic readings were a scam. I'd never believed in psychics before, but the reading had seemed so...well, so real. I stood up, feeling restless, but couldn't decide what to do. The room was quiet, and the air felt too still. Finally I sat back down, picked up the phone and dialed Joni's number.

"Hello?" Joni's voice sounded croaky.

"It's me. Did I wake you up?"

"No, no." She laughed and then coughed. "Well, yes. I was having a bit of a nap. But that's okay. You know I'm always happy to hear from you."

I relaxed. Hearing Joni's voice always made me feel better. "Um...I went to the marina after school."

"Did you?" Joni's voice was neutral. She knew I wasn't supposed to go there. She also knew that I needed to. Mostly I didn't mention my visits to the marina because Joni told me she didn't want to have secrets from my dad, but I needed to talk to someone.

"Um, Joni..." My voice was suddenly thick, and I had to swallow hard and clench my teeth to hold back tears. "There was a For Sale sign on *Eliza J.*"

Joni waited for a long moment before she answered. "Oh dear," she said at last. "Oh dear. I've been wondering when this would happen."

"You have?"

"I'm surprised he's hung on to the boat for as long as he has, love. You know how much it costs to keep a boat in the water."

Actually, I didn't have a clue. "Maybe I could pay. If I got a job after school or something."

"Honey, it's hundreds of dollars a month. There's no way you can cover that with babysitting. In any case, I don't imagine it's only about the money."

"Mom loved that boat," I said fiercely. "He's got no right to sell it."

"Oh, Fiona."

I lay down on the bed and closed my eyes. Joni sounded so sad. "She was your sister," I said. "You know how important sailing was to her."

"I know how important sailing was to you," Joni said softly.

Everyone did that: changed the subject whenever I tried to talk about Mom. "You all want to forget about Mom, don't you? That's why Dad's selling the boat."

"Fiona! How can you say that? Of course we don't." Her voice cracked, and she started coughing and coughing. "Listen," she said after she caught her breath. "No one wants to forget your mother."

I didn't say anything. That sure wasn't how it seemed to me.

four

Dad looked up as I entered the living room. "Um, Dad?"

"Fiona. Good. I was about to come and find you." He cleared his throat. "There's something I want to talk to you about."

Was he going to tell me about selling *Eliza J*? I held my breath and waited.

Dad sat down in his armchair and ran his hands through his hair. He didn't have a lot of it, and he combed it over the bald spot on top of his head. Mom always used to say he should shave his head, and I had to agree. Half the time, his hair was hanging the wrong way, and it didn't cover the bald patch anyway.

He gestured for me to sit, and I perched on one arm of the couch. I wondered if he was feeling bad about putting the boat up for sale without even talking to me about it. "What is it?" I asked him.

He cleared his throat again and looked so miserable that I was almost tempted to tell him that I already knew. Almost. "The thing is…Well, I've been meaning to say something about this for a while. I suppose I should have brought it up sooner." He looked at me a little desperately.

"So why didn't you?" I had to concentrate on keeping my voice steady.

"I guess I've been worried about how you'd react." Dad leaned toward me. "Honey…"

"I already know."

He looked relieved. "You do? You guessed?"

I opened my mouth to explain, but Dad kept talking, his words coming out in a rush. "We've been seeing each other for a couple of months, but I wasn't ready for anything too serious. I wasn't planning to get involved with anyone, but she's a wonderful woman, and I know you'll like her."

I stared at him. "*What?*"

"I want you to meet her." His neck was getting red and blotchy.

"You…you're saying you have a…you're dating someone?"

He nodded and frowned. "I thought you said you already knew."

I pushed my fists against my stomach, hard, as if this would stop everything from spilling out. "No. I was thinking of something else. Not that."

"Well." There was a pause. "I thought we could all have dinner together one night. With her daughter. She's about your age."

"Dinner?"

"So you can get to know her. Them. Both of them."

There was a lump in my throat. *What about Mom?* "I don't want to get to know them," I said out loud.

"Don't be like that, Fi."

"Like what? I'm not being like anything." I stood up. "I'm just not interested in meeting this...this...your..."

"Her name's Katherine."

Katherine. I hated her already. Trying to shove her way into our lives. Trying to make Dad forget all about Mom. Images flickered through my mind. Snapshots. Mom sitting on the couch, doing a crossword puzzle and laughing at a story I was telling her. Mom standing tall at the helm of our boat, the wind whipping her long hair back. Mom's hand gripping mine as we peered over the edge of the dock, looking at—what? A fish, maybe? A sea star? I couldn't remember. "I don't want to meet her," I said again.

Dad cleared his throat. He took off his glasses and wiped them on his shirt. "Well...I'll give you some time to get used to the idea."

I just stared at him. Then I turned around and ran up the stairs to my bedroom.

*
· *
* *

The next morning, Dad said Joni was feeling better and I could go to her place after school as usual.

I nodded. "I have to leave early," I told him. "I have a group project meeting before class." It wasn't true, but I didn't even feel a twinge of guilt about lying to him.

I waved as I walked out the door, got on my bike and headed straight to the marina.

*
· *
* *

I stepped aboard *Eliza J* and walked up to the bow. When Mom and I were sailing, I liked to sit up here if I wasn't at the helm. Sometimes, when I was younger, I used to bring along a coloring book and a pack of markers, or a book to read, but most of the time I just dangled my feet over the side of the boat and listened to the sounds of the wind in the rigging and the water rushing past the hull.

I held onto the forestay and looked around the marina and out toward the sea. A small red-hulled sailboat was making its way into the marina. Maybe a twenty-one or twenty-three footer, with a single mast, cluttered deck and an outboard engine. Lucky people, to be out sailing instead of spending the day in school.

A few months ago, I'd asked Dad if I could crew on one of the racing boats that sailed out of here every Wednesday night, all year round. But Dad had practically choked on his breakfast cereal. I didn't want to bring it up again. Joni said he couldn't stand to think about anything happening to me, but that was stupid. Sailing wasn't that dangerous, especially around here. What happened to Mom was just bad luck. Besides, if Mom had been on *Eliza J* instead of her friend's lightweight fin-keeled boat, I bet she'd have been okay. She'd always said *Eliza J* was a boat she'd trust with her life.

I still hadn't told Dad I knew about our boat being for sale. I didn't want to talk to him. I didn't even want to be around him. Or his—what? Girlfriend? He was too old for a girlfriend. I didn't know what to call her.

* * *

I was almost late again. I walked into the classroom at 8:45 and slipped into the seat beside Abby.

She turned to me. "You're late again."

I looked up at the clock just as the second bell rang. "No, I'm not."

She rolled her eyes. "Uh-huh."

"Okay, okay. Almost late. But listen, I have to talk to you."

Mrs. Moskin walked in, and the room fell silent.

"After class," I mouthed.

The teacher caught my eye, cleared her throat meaningfully and launched us right into geometry. Ugh.

I flipped open my book and did my best to concentrate. I couldn't afford not to. Mrs. Moskin and I don't see eye to eye. Abby says that she and I have opposite personality types. She says I'm an ISTJ—introverted, sensing, thinking, judging—and Mrs. Moskin is an ENFP—extroverted, intuiting, feeling, perceiving. Abby wants to be a psychologist, so she's forever analyzing everyone and trying to make them take tests or fill out questionnaires. She tried to get Joni and Tom to do them once, but they just laughed, and Tom said he was RFCB: Ready For a Cold Beer.

I stared at the page and blew out a sigh. Even if I could convince Dad to keep *Eliza J*, he'd never let me sail her. When I was old enough to do what I wanted, I'd get my own boat, maybe like the little red one I saw that morning. I wouldn't mind having a boat like that. Not too big, easy to sail single-handed.

Even with the clutter on the deck, you could see that the boat had nice lines.

I doodled a picture of *Eliza J* on the inside cover of my binder. *Eliza J*, I wrote, curling the end of the *J* into a little circle like a neatly coiled dock line. No boat could ever replace *Eliza J*.

At lunch, I finally got a chance to tell Abby what had happened. "Sit down," I told her.

Abby obediently slid down to the floor, her back against her locker.

I squatted in front of her. "You're not going to believe this."

Abby raised her eyebrows and waited.

"It's Dad," I said. "He's seeing someone. A woman." I waited to see how she'd respond.

She opened her eyes so wide I could see white all around her brown irises. "Really? You're not joking?"

I shook my head. "I wish."

There was a long pause.

Abby rested her elbows on her knees and balanced her chin on her hands. "Wow. Tedium."

"Yeah. It sucks. I can't believe it."

She hesitated. "Though…well, maybe it'll be all right, you know? Maybe you'll like her."

I stared at her. "I'm not going to like her, okay?"

"Aw, come on, Fi. You don't want your dad to be single forever, do you?"

I thought about that for about three seconds. "Yeah, actually, I'd be okay with that."

She gave a half-laugh, but she was still frowning. "My dad's seeing someone. Well, you met his girlfriend, remember?"

"That's different," I said. "Your mother isn't dead."

Most people changed the subject when I used the D word, but Abby didn't even flinch. "Why's it different?"

"Because. It just is."

"Fi? Are you...okay?" Abby put her hand on my arm.

"He's selling the boat," I whispered. "Mom's boat."

"Oh." She winced. "That sucks. I mean, really sucks. Beyond tedium."

I nodded and said nothing.

"I guess it sort of makes sense though. No one was using it anymore."

"I was."

"Yeah. Sort of. But..." Abby broke off. "Does your dad even know you still go down there? You're not allowed to, right?"

I shook my head. "No. He says it's not good for me. He says it's"—I tried to remember his word—"morbid. It's so stupid. Like he thinks I sit on the boat, getting depressed and thinking about Mom being dead."

Abby said nothing for a moment, and I wondered if that was what she thought too. "I guess he's trying to do what he thinks is best," she said.

I didn't know what Abby's problem was. Lately she seemed to be on everyone's side but mine.

five

After school I rode over to Joni's. Her house is on a quiet little dead-end street, halfway between my house and the marina. I locked my bike to her fence and let myself in.

Joni was in the kitchen, perched on a stool, with a mug of tea in one hand. The kitchen was the main living area in her house: a big, sunny room with pine cupboards and bookshelves, terracotta floor, shiny pots and pans hanging from big hooks on the ceiling, and a wild jungle of plants tumbling leafy green limbs across the cluttered countertops.

Joni is my mom's older sister. Fifteen years older, actually—people sometimes think she's my grandmother. She isn't one of those people who try to look young. She let her hair go gray years ago, and it's long and curly and kind of wild. And she's quite fat. She doesn't believe in diets. She says that they make people obsess about food and get even fatter.

She looked up as I walked in. "Look at this," she said. Her voice was low and scratchy from being sick. "I was thinking about taking a course up at the university." She held up a glossy catalogue.

I made a face. "No way would I do school if I didn't have to."

She ignored me. "Pottery classes," she said, flipping pages. "And look at this—Southeast Asian literature! And here, there are courses on astronomy! Listen to this: 'An introduction to astronomy, covering constellations, planetary motion, recent discoveries about planets, pulsars, black holes, galaxies and cosmology. The evening labs will allow students to use telescopes and to analyze data.' Now doesn't that sound fascinating?"

"I guess."

Joni put down the catalogue and took off her reading glasses. Hot pink cat's-eye glasses. "Want to talk about it?"

I pulled a stool up to the counter beside her. "It's Dad," I said. "He's seeing someone."

"I know. He called me last night and told me about Katherine. He said you were upset."

I nodded. "Understatement."

"Is it really so bad?"

I looked away from her sympathetic half smile, glared down at the green swirls of the countertop and concentrated on not crying. "It's like he's forgetting about Mom."

"Like I told you last night, no one's going to be forgetting your mom. Not ever." Joni put a soft arm around my shoulders. "Do you need a snack? I made some great peanut-butter cookies."

Joni's cookies are incredible. And I'm kind of a peanut-butter addict. "Okay."

She winked at me, slipped off her stool and padded barefoot over to the fridge. Standing on her tiptoes, she grabbed a tin from the top of the fridge and plunked it down in front of me. She poured me a tall glass of milk and sat back down.

"Things are okay otherwise?" she asked.

I thought about *Eliza J*, and about Abby and her hesitation about being my partner for the science project. And that math test. I'd have to tell Dad. "Not great," I said out loud. "Total tedium, actually."

Joni waited. I didn't say anything. We sat in silence for a moment, munching.

After a minute, Joni opened her mouth and closed it again.

"What?" I asked.

She hesitated. "Do you want to know what I think?"

I nodded.

"I think your dad is someone who isn't good at being alone. I think he's been very lonely without Jennifer." Joni took a second cookie out of the tin, looked at it thoughtfully and put it back again. "I have to stop eating these."

"So maybe he should learn to be alone."

"Maybe." She blew her nose on a big pink handkerchief and tucked it back in her pocket. "Peter doesn't find it easy to meet people. He's not the type to go out a lot. He's not good at small talk. How did he meet this Katherine, by the way?"

"I don't know." It hadn't occurred to me to wonder, but it was a good question. "Did you talk to him about the boat?"

I shook my head.

"You should." Joni picked up another cookie. "Maybe just one more."

Dad picked me up from Joni's at five and wrestled my bike into the back of his car. He was dressed up in a shirt and tie, and he kept humming to himself while he drove. He didn't seem to notice that I was not sharing his mood.

"Fiona," he said. "I have a surprise for you."

I tensed. "What?" I didn't like surprises. I didn't trust them.

"I'm taking you out to dinner," he said. "Your favorite. Paul's Pizza Palace."

I relaxed. Paul's Pizza Palace looked like a dive, but it had the best pizza in town. "Oh. Cool." Maybe he was trying to make up for last night.

He cleared his throat, and I knew exactly what he was going to say before he even began. "Katherine and her daughter are going to meet us there."

"Dad…"

He held up one hand. "No. No, Fiona. Don't start. I want you to meet them."

I spoke slowly, emphasizing each word. "And I. Don't. Want. To."

"Oh, Fiona. Please don't be like that. Katherine and I have been spending some time together and—"

I interrupted. "Fine." I spat the word out. "That doesn't mean I have to."

"Fi, come on. I'm trying to include you. Can't you…can't you give them a chance?"

I turned away from him and stared out the car window. "It's only been a year," I whispered.

Dad didn't say anything. We drove in silence. Eventually Dad parallel-parked down the street from Paul's Pizza Palace and turned off the engine. He unbuckled his seatbelt and started to get out.

"It's like you're trying to erase Mom," I told him, not moving.

"Of course I'm not." He sat back down, looking shocked. "That's ridiculous."

"I know about *Eliza J*, Dad. I know you're trying to get rid of her too."

"How did you…?" He looked at his watch. "This is not a good time to have this conversation."

"Oh no, we wouldn't want to keep them waiting," I said sarcastically.

He shook his head. "I was going to tell you. There is no point in keeping a boat that no one uses. It costs a small fortune in marina fees." He put his hand on my knee and looked at me, a hopeful half smile on his face. "Hey, Fifi? You know what a boat is?"

"What?"

"A boat's a hole in the water into which you pour money."

I pulled my knee away. "Hilarious."

The tentative grin slipped off his face, and I felt a flicker of remorse. Dad used to joke all the time, but he hardly ever did anymore.

He sighed. "We can talk about this later. What were you doing at the marina, anyway? I told you I didn't want you hanging around there."

I didn't say a word. Mom was right: Dad didn't understand anything at all.

Paul's Pizza Palace was where I celebrated everything from birthdays to soccer wins. I nearly always sat at my favorite booth: the one in the back corner with the picture of dogs playing pool hanging on the wall beside it. And I nearly always ordered the same thing: Hawaiian, double pineapple, extra cheese. Everything about the place was familiar, right down to the strips of duct tape covering the cracks in the red vinyl benches.

I guess Dad picked this restaurant because I liked it, but that made it even worse. We all used to come here together: me and him and Mom. When I was little, like six or seven, I used to get plain cheese pizza, no sauce, and I'd bring markers and color on the paper placemats while we waited for the food to come. I remember how Dad used to ask the server for extra placemats because he said my artwork was too beautiful to spill food on, and I remember how he and Mom used to hold hands right on top of the table.

This was the last place I wanted to come with my father and his new girlfriend. I still didn't know what to call her. Words like *boyfriend* and *girlfriend* seemed kind of stupid when you're talking about people as old as my dad.

I hung back, and Dad walked in ahead of me, looking around. He turned to me. "Look at that. Katherine picked your favorite table."

Reluctantly, I looked toward the back corner of the restaurant—and gasped.

It was her. The psychic woman from the Mystic Heart shop.

I couldn't move. Every muscle in my body seemed to have seized up.

"Come on," Dad said over his shoulder. "What are you waiting for?"

I let my breath out in a long *whoosh*—breathe, breathe—and forced myself to follow him. The psychic woman—Katherine—and her daughter were sitting on opposite sides of the booth. Dad squeezed in beside Katherine, and I reluctantly slid onto the bench beside her daughter, staring down at the table to avoid meeting anyone's eyes. My heart was racing. I wondered if Katherine would tell Dad that she'd already met me. I sure wasn't going to mention it.

I snuck a sideways glance at Katherine's daughter as I sat down. Dad had said she was my age, but she looked younger. She had very straight pale blond hair, and her cheeks were pink and she was all big-eyed and silent, her mouth hanging open in a way that made her look kind of stunned and stupid.

I nodded at her and snuck a peek across the table at Katherine. She was wearing the same blue and white snowflake sweater she had worn at the Mystic Heart, but her hair was twisted up in some kind of clip. Younger than Dad, who was in his fifties; younger than Mom too. She saw me looking at her and gave me a quick smile. If she recognized me, she wasn't letting on. "I'm Kathy," she said. "And you must be Fiona."

My mother had hated nicknames. She always introduced herself as Jennifer and quickly corrected anyone who called her Jenny. She said nicknames were fine for under-twelves, but adults who hung on to names like Bobby and Mikey and Kathy and Jenny were trying to avoid growing up. She called me Fi, but I guessed maybe it was different with your own kid. She was always telling me not to grow up too fast.

"And this is my daughter Caitlin," Kathy said after she gave up waiting for me to reply. "She's twelve."

I'd have guessed ten, or maybe eleven, tops.

"And you're thirteen, aren't you, Fiona?"

If she already knew, why was she asking? She already had way too much information about me. I hated that she'd seen me cry: just the thought made me feel hot and angry. "Yes," I said. "How old are you?"

She glanced at Dad, laughing.

Dad frowned at me. "Fiona." There was a warning in his voice.

"She asked me," I protested.

"It's fine, Peter. Really." Kathy's cheeks turned as pink as Caitlin's, but her voice stayed calm. "I just turned forty. The big four-oh."

"That's how old my dad was when I was born," I told her. "So he's thirteen years older than you."

Dad looked embarrassed. "Yes, Fiona. Thanks for pointing that out."

My mom was six years younger than Dad. It didn't sound like much of an age difference, but it had sometimes seemed like he was a whole generation older: all hung up on teaching me responsibility, getting angry about Mom letting me skip school to go sailing, wearing the same awful old pair of high-waisted Wrangler jeans with the big yellow *W* stitched on the pocket. Mom wasn't very interested in fashion either, but she wouldn't have been caught dead— I caught my breath and dragged my mind back to the conversation before the whirlpool could suck me in. "Well, thirteen years is a lot," I said, shrugging. "It's my entire lifetime."

Kathy gave me a steady look. Her eyes were dark and deep-set, with faint blue-gray shadows beneath them. She didn't have a lot of wrinkles or anything, but her eyes looked older than forty.

I squirmed under her gaze. I was pretty sure she must recognize me.

"Well," she said at last. "So. You're thirteen. I do remember that age, though sometimes I'd prefer not to." She smiled. "Tell me about yourself, Fiona. What are you interested in?"

"What am I *interested* in?" I repeated.

She looked uncomfortable. "Yes. You know, hobbies or sports, maybe? Caitlin does gymnastics and plays the flute."

"Used to play the flute," Caitlin mumbled.

"And she takes dance classes, so I wondered what you were interested in."

I shrugged. "Sailing."

"Oh. Really? But…" Her voice trailed off.

"She doesn't sail," Dad said flatly.

"Not anymore. Because you won't let me. Because you're selling Mom's boat." My voice was a little too loud.

He looked around a little frantically and signaled to the server. "Do you all know what you want? Can we just order?"

"Peter." Kathy reached out a hand toward my father and smiled at him. I couldn't help noticing that her teeth were kind of crooked. "It's all right. I think we should expect this to be a little awkward."

The waiter appeared beside our table. "Hey, gang. Having a good night?"

I glanced up at him. Tall, skinny, a whole bunch of piercings in his lips and eyebrows and chin. I hadn't seen him here before, and I hoped he didn't think we were all one family. Yuck, yuck, yuck.

"You ready to order?"

"Hawaiian, extra pineapple, extra cheese," I said quickly.

"Oh! Hawaiian is my favorite too." Kathy looked like this was the most exciting thing ever. "We can share one."

"Actually, I've changed my mind," I said. "I'd rather have the vegetarian special."

Dad gave me a long look and shook his head before turning to Caitlin. "And what about you, Caitlin? Do you know what you want?"

"I can share the vegetarian pizza with Fiona," she whispered, and she gave me this sappy little smile, as if she thought I might like her just because she agreed to eat the same kind of pizza as me.

I picked at a piece of duct tape holding the bench seat together and wondered if Dad had any idea what he was getting himself into. Did he know his new girl-friend was a psychic? Or claimed to be one, at least? I peeked at Kathy again from beneath my lowered eyelashes. She didn't look like a psychic. She looked totally ordinary, like she should be a teacher or an accountant or a receptionist. Something normal.

"Okay, so the kids can share the vegetarian. Kathy and I will have the Hawaiian and two glasses of the house red," Dad told the waiter. "Coke, kids?"

"Sure," Caitlin whispered. "Thanks."

"Water's fine for me," I said. *Kids.* Did he actually want the waiter to think we were a family?

six

I hate olives and I hate green peppers, which was mostly what seemed to be on the vegetarian pizza. I picked them off and piled them on the edge of my plate. Across the table, Kathy kept smiling at me over her gooey pineapple and ham pizza. I didn't know what I was supposed to be feeling. I'd liked her when I met her before, but knowing that she was dating my father changed everything.

"So, Fiona," she said. "You must be in grade seven, right?"

"Right."

"And…how is school?"

"Fine."

Dad glared at me, but I didn't know what I was doing wrong. So I wasn't falling all over myself to make conversation. Last I heard, that wasn't a major crime. And besides, like Abby said, I was an ISTJ. I for Introverted. So I was supposed to be a little reserved.

He leaned toward me, eyebrows pulled close together. "Fiona. That is enough."

I looked back innocently. "Enough?"

"You're being rude, and it is not acceptable."

Anger flashed somewhere behind my eyes, bright white and blistering. I felt like he'd just slapped me right in front of Kathy and Caitlin. Fine. He wanted polite? I'd show him I could be as phony as they were. And I could let out Kathy's little secret in the process. "So, *Kathy*. What do you do? Tell me a little about yourself." I smiled at Dad. "Better?"

He didn't smile back. "Much."

Kathy laughed. "Oh, well, I'm not that interesting. I moved here three years ago, when Caitlin was in fourth grade. After her father passed."

Passed. Like he did okay on an exam or something. I hate it when people use words like that. I never say Mom *passed*. She died. Died, died, dead. Also, Kathy laughed too much. There wasn't anything that funny going on, as far as I could see.

I thought of the way Mom used to laugh: full-on, head-thrown-back laughter. Joni laughed like that too, sometimes so hard she'd actually snort. It might not be the politest laugh, but I'd give anything to hear my mom laugh again. I shook off the thought. "So what do you do? I mean, for work?" I could hardly wait to see Dad's reaction when she said she was a psychic. He hated that kind of thing. He was even scornful of people who read their horoscopes in the paper. Mom used to call him narrow-minded, and he would snort and say that if refusing to believe in superstition and new-age nonsense made him narrow-minded, then that was fine with him.

"Actually, I'm a medium." Kathy shrugged, as if this was a perfectly normal thing to say.

I stared at her. Small, medium, large. All that came to mind was pizza or clothing. "A medium?"

"Yes. I bring messages from those on the other side—from those who have gone on to a higher plane."

I glanced at Dad, but he didn't look upset. He didn't even look surprised. "Dead people," I said flatly, wanting to make sure he understood what Kathy was saying. I wondered why she hadn't let on that she'd met me already. Did she think Dad would be angry? Or was there some code of privacy, like with a counselor or a priest or something? Then again, she'd probably done about a hundred readings that day at the shop; maybe she didn't remember me at all.

"From the departed, yes. I do readings too—auras, Tarot, dream interpretation. It depends on what the client's needs are."

She said it like she thought I might be impressed, but I was thinking about what Abby had said: *It's all acting and guesswork.* I remembered the palm reader at the fair confidently informing my mom that she had a long life line. Another good actor, but not such a good guess. "Do you read palms?" I asked slowly.

Her face lit up. "Would you like me to look at yours sometime?" She glanced at Dad. "If it's okay with your father?"

"No, thanks." I pushed myself along the slippery bench seat and stood up. "Excuse me. I have to go to the washroom." Ignoring the roaring in my ears, I walked as fast as I could past the rows of red-and-white-checked tablecloths and into the safety of the ladies room. I slammed the cubicle door and locked it behind me. Safe. I leaned against the door, feeling its cool smooth metal, and started to cry. How could Dad do this?

A few minutes later, someone knocked at the door. "Fiona?"

It was her. "Go away." I didn't want her to hear me crying.

"Your dad wanted me to check on you. He can't come in the ladies room. He wanted to make sure you were okay."

I pushed my hands against my mouth and didn't answer.

"Fiona? Can you...Just tell me if..." Her voice trailed off.

"I'm fine." I choked out the words. I could still hear her stepping closer to the stall door, testing it to see if it was locked.

"Fiona." She lowered her voice. "Look, I didn't mention Saturday to your father. The reading, you know?"

"I thought maybe you didn't recognize me."

"Of course, I recognized you. I'd been thinking about you, actually. I was a bit worried about how you reacted to the reading. When you walked in with your father tonight, I put the pieces together. I'm so sorry, Fiona."

Sorry my mother was dead? Sorry she'd had some crazy psychic vision of my mom's last hours alive? Or sorry she'd lied to me and made the whole thing up?

"I felt so uncomfortable about it." Kathy cleared her throat. "And I didn't know if you had told your father about the reading."

"Are you kidding? He'd freak out."

Kathy sighed. "Oh, dear. What a mess. I should have said something right away, but I wanted to respect your privacy."

"No. Don't tell him."

"Why not, Fiona? It doesn't seem right to keep this a secret."

"He'll freak out. I'm serious." I balled my hands into fists and pushed them against my thighs. "Anyway, I wouldn't have talked to you if I'd known you were… if I'd known you knew my dad."

Kathy didn't say anything right away. I was starting to wonder if she was still there when she said, "I won't say anything if you don't want me to, but I'm sure he wouldn't be angry. I think you should tell him yourself. Especially if you're still feeling upset or confused about the reading."

I snorted. "As if. Abby and I only went into that shop for a laugh. It's not like I believe in any of that stuff." I felt a sharp twinge as I said it: What if Kathy was right, and Mom was still around? Could she even be listening right now? She might not try to get in touch with me if she thought I wasn't even open to the idea.

"That's fine, then." Kathy hesitated; then she spoke softly. "I do know something about grief, Fiona."

Like I wanted to hear about her problems. "Whatever," I said.

"I know it might seem hard to believe right now, but it will get easier for you."

"Right." If she really wanted to make it easier for me, she could start by staying away from my father.

"Come back to the table when you are ready, okay?"

I didn't answer. After a few seconds, I heard her leave.

It will get easier. Yeah, right. Sure, there were moments of feeling okay: sitting in classes at school, eating dinner at Joni's, laughing about stuff with Abby. Moments when I forgot about Mom being dead. No, not forgot about it, but just didn't think about it for a while. And I'd be having fun, and then I'd remember Mom and feel worse than ever. Because how could I be having fun when my mom was dead and would never have fun again?

Mom was all about having fun. *Life's too short to waste time on things you don't enjoy,* she said one time when Dad complained about his job.

Dad had rolled his eyes. *Someone has to pay the bills, Jennifer.*

Dad was a high-school principal, and Mom was a substitute teacher. They actually met at a teachers' conference. But in the last couple of years, Mom had been too busy sailing to work very much. She always checked the weather forecast before she decided whether or not to be available to teach the next day.

Mom was one of those people you couldn't help liking. She had this wide smile that made everyone else smile too; it was infectious in the same way yawns are. And I couldn't believe—I just could not believe—that I was never going to see her smile again. I started crying, arms wrapped around myself, rocking back and forth. Remembering hurt too much.

Even my happiest memories pulled me into a whirl-pool of guilt.

Because I had taken Mom's side. *Stop trying to tell her what to do all the time,* I said to Dad. *She knows what she's doing. You don't even know how to sail.*

My father must hate me. I pushed my hands against my mouth and tried to muffle the sound of my crying. I tried taking deep breaths, but it wasn't working. I couldn't catch my breath—it was like my throat was partially closed off or something. I started crying in this hiccupy kind of way, in noisy gasps that hurt my chest.

There was another knock on my cubicle door. "Fiona, honey?"

Dad, in the ladies room. I tried again to take a deep breath, and this time the air went down more easily. "Dad?"

"Listen, honey. You have to stop doing this to yourself."

"I'm not doing anything," I gasped out. I pushed my hands against my chest. "I just…I just…"

"Can you please come out of there?" I heard a door open, and a woman's voice said, "Oh, excuse me."

I opened the door. Dad smiled apologetically at the woman and put his arm around me, pulling me out of the ladies room and into the tiny hallway. He rubbed my back. "Oh, honey."

I was still crying, but it wasn't the panicky-can't-breathe type anymore—just the regular kind of tears. "I want to go home."

"Take a few minutes and calm yourself down, okay? Then we'll finish our dinner and…"

"I'm not eating with her."

Dad looked at me, his hair flopping the wrong way and his shoulders lifting helplessly. "Fiona. Please. This is important to me."

I didn't know how he could even stand to be in the same room with her. Anger flashed through me like electricity, and I stopped crying abruptly. "Come on, Dad. She says she talks to dead people."

"Fiona. Don't be so closed-minded."

I thought about what Kathy had said back at the Mystic Heart—the waves, the darkness, the feeling of fear. "Do you believe her?" I rubbed my eyes with my sleeve, harder than necessary. "You can't believe her, Dad. That's crazy."

He took off his glasses and polished the lenses on his shirt, not looking at me. "I don't know, Fiona. Who's to say it isn't possible?"

I wanted to believe it was possible. I really did. I'd give anything to talk to my mother again. But wanting to believe something didn't make it true. I couldn't stand to see Dad being taken in by Kathy's lies. "Me," I said fiercely. "And anyone who isn't a total idiot." I reached up and snapped my fingers in front of his eyes. "Dad. One. Two. Three. You are waking up now. Open your eyes."

He swatted my hand away. "What are you doing?"

"I thought maybe she'd hypnotized you," I said.

"Don't be smart. This isn't funny." He put his glasses back on.

"You're telling me."

We stared at each other for a long minute. Dad's face was creased with fury, and for a second I thought I'd gone too far. His Adam's apple jumped as he swallowed. "Fiona." He took a deep breath and blew it out slowly, as if he was trying to calm himself down. "I know it was probably a shock to find out I was dating, if that's the right thing to call it. But I don't understand why you got so upset, why you rushed off like that."

"You don't?" I raised my voice slightly. "Seriously? You don't know?" My stomach hurt, and I folded my arms across it.

"Fiona, come back to the table. Whatever is going on with you, well, you can be angry with me if you want to, but it isn't fair to Caitlin and Kathy to take it out on them."

I hesitated.

"Now." Dad lowered his chin and met my eyes. "Right now."

Obviously, I didn't have a choice. I followed him back to the booth and slid back in beside Caitlin like nothing had happened. She was even more wide-eyed and stunned-looking than before.

"It'll be okay," Kathy said, like she was trying to be reassuring. "You'll see."

Did the spirits tell you that, Kathy? I bit my tongue and said nothing. I wasn't so sure that everything would be okay. My hopes on that subject were not high at all. In fact, they were somewhere down around the fallen pieces of pepperoni on the black-and-white-tiled floor. I sighed. For now, I just had to get through the next couple of hours.

* * *

To my relief, everyone decided to ignore me, and they carried on with their meal as if I wasn't there. Every so often, I snuck a peek at Kathy. I couldn't believe Dad had actually fallen for someone who claimed to speak with dead people. I couldn't believe he'd fallen for someone who told lies for a living.

seven

The awful dinner at Paul's Pizza Palace ended eventually. I looked away as Dad said goodbye to Kathy, all awkward handshakes and shoulder pats, like he wanted to kiss her, but not in front of me. He tousled Caitlin's hair. "Bye, kiddo."

Kiddo was what Tom called me, but I'd never heard Dad say it before. It looked like he already knew Caitlin well enough to be on a pet-name basis. Apparently, I was the only one who had been kept in the dark about Dad and Kathy's relationship.

"Bye, Fiona," Kathy said. "It was nice to meet you."

"Uh-huh." I kept my eyes lowered, embarrassed about having lost it earlier. They probably thought I was a drama queen. Then again, who cared what they thought?

Dad and I got in the car, and he drove toward home. Neither of us spoke until we were pulling into our driveway. Dad glanced at me and looked away again. He drummed his fingers on the steering wheel and fiddled with the windshield wipers, squirting washer fluid and cleaning the windshield even though it looked perfectly clean already. He turned off the engine and looked at me. His eyes were pink and tired-looking behind his wire-rimmed glasses.

"I guess I shouldn't have sprung it on you like that," he said. "Maybe you needed a little more warning. A little time to get used to the idea before you met them."

I felt flat and emptied out from crying. "Maybe." I didn't think I'd ever get used to the idea. I didn't even *want* to get used to it.

It was a relief to get up to my own room and shut the door behind me. It wasn't late but I changed into my pj's before lifting my mattress and sliding out the chart book I had hidden there. I sat cross-legged on my bed and spread the chart book open in front of me. I stared at the familiar pale blue background dotted with the tiny yellow shapes of the islands and swirled with contour lines. Somewhere in that pale blue expanse was my mother.

Dead reckoning. That's what it was called when you navigated without using a GPS or anything, without having landmarks or even the stars to look to. Dead reckoning meant finding your way by keeping track of your position based upon your speed, your compass course and the passing of time. I knew how to take a fix on a point of land; I knew how to plot my position and my course on a chart. Mom had taught me that. I also knew that when you were on the water, lots of things could throw you off. Tides, currents, drift. Even your watch running a few minutes slow, or the algae on your boat's hull interfering with your boat's knot meter so that you didn't gauge your speed accurately. You could end up miles from where you thought you were.

That's what we believed happened to Mom: a simple navigation error. She had flown down to French Polynesia to help a friend with a passage from Raiatea to another island, and they hit a reef in the middle of the night. They shouldn't have been anywhere near it. A GPS error, some people had suggested, but Mom would never have relied on GPS. She'd have been plotting her course the old-fashioned way. Another boat saw the flares they set off, but it was a rough night, and Mom's boat a long way from anywhere. It was the next morning before anyone could even start looking.

By that time, it was too late. The sailboat had been battered on the reef and completely destroyed. A couple of weeks later, their life raft was found hundreds of miles away. It had been inflated and released, but no one was in it.

They never found Mom or her friend.

I traced my finger over the lines around Raiatea. Sometimes I imagined that Mom was still out there somewhere, that she had washed up on some tropical shore and was surviving on coconuts, waiting to be rescued. Or maybe she'd been rescued by the islanders and was living with them, playing on a golden beach with their chubby laughing children and catching brightly colored fish and watching the waves rolling over the fine white sand. But I didn't really believe it.

I knew she wasn't ever coming home.

* * *

The next day at school, I grabbed Abby in the hallway before the morning bell rang.

"You are not going to believe this," I told her.

She raised one eyebrow. "What?"

"Dad made me go for dinner last night with the woman he's been seeing. And guess what? It was that woman from the Mystic Heart place."

"Are you serious?" Her mouth fell open in a perfect circle. "The owner or the psychic?"

"The psychic. Well, the one who claims to be psychic." I made a face. "Her name's Kathy."

"Yeah, I remember. That is so weird." Abby bit her lower lip and shook her head slowly. "Freaky weird."

"Tell me about it."

"I kind of thought you were taken in by that reading," she said. "When you wouldn't talk about it, you know?"

"Yeah, I know." I shrugged. "But I thought about it later. And I think you were right. She totally could've been just tossing words out. Waves could be anything. Microwaves, radio waves, a wave pool, waves of sadness, somebody waving." I stopped walking and let the rush of kids part around us on their way into the lunchroom. "What I can't believe is that Dad seems to be taken in by her lies. He's all, like, 'Well, Fiona, who's to say it isn't possible?'"

She winced. "Tedium. He doesn't seem the type to fall for that kind of scam."

The bell rang, and I looked Abby in the eyes. "Lunchtime," I said quickly. "We have to talk. And I have to come up with some kind of a plan to get her out of my life."

I don't think I heard a word Mrs. Moskin said that morning. All I could think about was how I could get rid of Kathy. Unfortunately, most of my ideas involved things like rare untraceable poisons, cliffs or zombies. None of which was very practical.

Finally we were set free, and Abby and I grabbed seats in the back corner of the lunchroom. Abby tipped her sandwich out of its plastic container: thick brown bread with seeds on the crust and leafy bits sticking out. The kind of sandwich my mom used to make. Dad mostly buys packaged things, like Baby Bel cheeses, and applesauce or pudding, and those little containers of crackers with cheese spread. When he makes sandwiches, they're plain peanut butter or gross greasy salami on thin squares of supermarket bread.

"Fiona? Earth to Fiona?"

I looked up. "Sorry. What?"

"I've been thinking about this all morning. Listen, I know it isn't likely, but what if Kathy really can do stuff? You know? Like talking to spirits or whatever. People who've died."

Like your mother. She didn't say the words, but I knew we were both thinking them. If Kathy was for real, maybe I could actually find out what had happened to Mom. Maybe I could even talk to her again. I started to get a tight ache in my stomach. "She can't," I said shortly. "No one can." My breath caught in my throat, and that panicky feeling started building up in my chest. I looked around the lunchroom: dozens of kids eating, talking, laughing. Acting normal. Sometimes I felt like there was a thick wall of glass between me and the rest of the world.

Abby looked at me. "Are you okay?"

I nodded. *I'm okay, I'm okay, I'm okay. Deep breaths.* My breathing eased, and the panicky feeling started to recede. "I don't believe in any of it," I said flatly.

"Yeah, I guess I don't either. Not really."

"Mom and I saw a palm reader once," I told her. "Did I ever tell you that? Last year, at the fall fair in Sidney?"

"You did? I thought they just had horses and pigs. Well, and rides and stuff."

"And this woman. Joanna something-or-other."

Abby looked curious. "And? What did she say?"

"She said that Mom had a long life line." I couldn't read Abby's expression. She was looking at me, head tilted, but not saying anything. "Well, so obviously she was a fake," I said. "You can't ask for clearer proof than that."

Abby nodded slowly. "I guess that doesn't prove they all are though. Right? It doesn't say anything about Kathy either way."

"I don't care. The only tricks I'm interested in seeing Kathy do are disappearing tricks. Poof. And her stupid kid too." I put down my half-eaten sandwich and peeled the lid off a pudding container. "I can't believe Dad's doing this to me."

"It is kind of weird that he'd pick someone so flaky."

"Yeah, I know. He doesn't usually go for that kind of thing. He's always made fun of people who read their horoscopes. I mean, he used to teach *science*. And he's always said he's an agnostic because there's no proof either way of God's existence."

"An agnostic? Is that like an atheist?"

"Sort of. It's saying you don't know whether there's a god or not. He says it's unknowable. Atheists believe there is no god, which is what I think. Well, most of the time at least." I licked the back of my plastic spoon. "Dad and Tom used to go on and on about this stuff."

We used to spend most Thursday nights together: me, Mom, Dad, Joni and Tom. We'd have dinner and play Balderdash or Labyrinth or Pictionary, Dad and Tom would argue about philosophical things, and I'd be allowed to stay up late. But since Mom died, that's fallen apart too. I see Joni and Tom a lot, but Dad never seems to want to go over there anymore.

Abby fiddled with a piece of lettuce that had fallen from her sandwich. "I believe in God. It's something you're supposed to take on faith, right?"

I had never understood how Abby, who was so logical about everything else, could make this one exception. She went to church every Sunday and to a Christian camp for two weeks every summer. When we were little, she used to say her prayers before she went to sleep; and I suddenly wondered if she still did. It wasn't the kind of thing you could ask someone. "Dad doesn't usually take anything on faith," I said instead. "He's all about evidence."

She shrugged and popped the lettuce in her mouth. "I guess he must believe Kathy's for real though."

"I don't know. I guess so."

"Well, I'm assuming. He wouldn't want to be with someone he thought was lying, right?"

I didn't know how to make sense of Dad and Kathy. I spooned the pudding into my mouth slowly, letting it melt into a warm sweet liquid on my tongue. If Dad believed her, wouldn't he want to try to speak to Mom? But if Kathy had actually given Dad a message from Mom, surely he'd have told me.

Abby took my silence as agreement. "And we know her psychic thing has to be phony, right? I mean, she isn't actually talking to dead people or predicting the future or whatever."

"Obviously." I couldn't see how any of this was helping. There was a long depressing silence. Kathy was a liar, Dad was stupid if he believed her, and I was stuck with a big phony in my life whether I liked it or not. I couldn't believe Dad had been taken in. If only…I gasped. "Abby!"

"What?"

"I've got the best idea." And it didn't involve poison, cliffs or zombies.

She looked apprehensive. "What is it?"

"Well, like you said, Dad wouldn't want to be with her if he thought she was a fraud. If he realized she was making all this stuff up."

"Maybe." Abby balanced a plastic container lid on one edge and tried to spin it around.

It skittered across the table toward me, and I put my hand down on it hard, like swatting a fly. "What do you mean, *maybe*?"

She shrugged. "If he likes her, you might be stuck with her anyway."

No way was I letting that happen. "If we prove she's a fake, Dad will have to forget about her."

Abby's eyes widened. "What if we did that for our science project? Mrs. Moskin said anything was okay as long as we had a hypothesis that we could prove or disprove."

I snorted. "Yeah, I can really see her going for this. 'Oh, Mrs. Moskin? Our hypothesis is that my dad's girlfriend is a big liar.'"

She shook her head impatiently. "We wouldn't word it quite like that, obviously. Maybe...hmm." She drummed her fingers against the edge of the table.

Something occurred to me. "Abby! Does this mean you want to be partners?"

"We're always partners."

"I know, but you seemed like you weren't sure."

She shrugged. "It's just that grades are really important to me, and lately you haven't been so much into schoolwork. But we're still partners, Fi. I wouldn't want to work with anyone else."

One of the knots inside me loosened and untied itself. "I'll do my share of the work, don't worry."

"I'm not worried. If we do this topic, you'll be motivated, right? Success is all about motivation."

I rolled my eyes. "Quit analyzing me."

She ignored me. "What if our hypothesis was that predicting the future is not possible? Or that psychic, um, psychic phenomena can be explained by...I don't know. I think we need some books."

Maybe we really could find a way to prove that Kathy was a liar. A spark of hope flickered and caught, and suddenly the room seemed brighter. "Abby? You're a genius."

"Yeah, yeah. I know." After a moment, her grin faded and was replaced by an anxious frown.

"What now?"

"I just don't know if this is a good idea. I wasn't too sure about my dad dating either, but his girlfriend turned out to be okay."

"She's not pretending to channel dead people or read palms."

"You were upset about your Dad dating even before you knew who his girlfriend was," Abby pointed out. "I don't think you should do this, okay? For the record."

"Got it," I said. "For the record."

"It might not be as bad as you think," she said. "With Kathy and your dad, I mean. She actually seemed pretty nice to me. Maybe you just don't like changes."

"Abby!" Sometimes she drove me crazy. "Quit analyzing me already and help me figure out how to get rid of her."

"Okay, but Fiona…"

"I want her gone." I looked at Abby. "Poof."

She hesitated; then she sighed and nodded. "Poof."

eight

I considered stopping by the marina on my way to Joni's after school but decided not to. It might be officially spring, but it sure felt like winter. My hands were practically frozen to my bike's handlebars. Besides, the thought of seeing *Eliza J* with that For Sale sign on her depressed me. I couldn't see any way to convince Dad to let me keep her. Even if, by some miracle, she didn't sell, he'd never let me sail her again anyway.

It wasn't like Mom's accident was *Eliza J*'s fault. *Eliza J* was built back in the seventies, and she was strong and solidly made. Mom said that modern boats were so thin-hulled you could see the fiberglass flexing when you hit the waves. When we installed a new compass on *Eliza J*, she'd sawed a four-inch circle of fiberglass out of the bulkhead. *Look at this*, she'd said, holding it up triumphantly so that it glinted in the sunlight like a medal. *At least an inch thick. She may not be fast, our Eliza J, but she's damn near indestructible.*

Eliza J wouldn't have been battered apart on a reef. It'd take a bomb to smash her to bits. The boat Mom had been on in the South Pacific had just cracked like an eggshell on the edge of a mixing bowl.

Eliza J had never been south. The farthest Mom and I had sailed her was up to Desolation Sound a couple of summers ago. I swallowed hard, remembering waves lapping on rocky shores and snow-capped mountains towering against blue sky. We had hiked for hours, swum together in the icy water, run out shivering and laughing, scampered across the stones on our numb feet to find our beach towels. We'd watched bald eagles soaring overhead and otters feeding and seals poking their heads out of the still waters. In the evenings, we'd sat in *Eliza J*'s cozy cabin and played Crazy Eights and talked about all the trips we'd make in the future. *Hawaii*, Mom had said. *Maybe next year, or the year after.*

Maybe never, I thought, pushing the memories aside.

*
· * ·
* *

"Bad day?" Joni asked when I walked into the kitchen.

I shrugged. "I don't know."

"Don't want to talk about it?"

I didn't know what I wanted. I sat down on a stool, leaned my elbows on the counter and looked up at Joni. Her gray hair was a wild mass of frizz. She'd traded the hot pink reading glasses for a leopard-print pair that hung on a beaded chain around her neck. She didn't say anything. She just sat there and waited, like she had all the time in the world.

I had an urge to put my arms around her and lean my head against her big soft shoulder, but Joni's not the huggy type. She looks like she would be, but she isn't at all. Mom wasn't either. I blinked a little. "Did you know this woman Dad's seeing is a psychic? Or a medium, or something?" I made air quotes with my fingers and talked in a fake-spooky voice. "Messages from your dear departed. From those who have gone beyond."

"Peter mentioned the medium thing." Joni shifted on her stool and made a face. "You know I'm a bit of a skeptic when it comes to that sort of thing, but it takes all kinds, doesn't it? And who's to say that her beliefs are any stranger than anyone else's?"

I thought about telling Joni that I'd met Kathy before and that she'd done a reading for me, but I decided against it. If I described what Kathy had said—the waves, the flares, the fear—she might think Kathy really was psychic. "Believe me," I said, "they're stranger."

Tom popped his head into the kitchen. "What's stranger?" He was wearing bright green plaid flannel pajamas with his ratty old housecoat untied over top.

Tom is the man Joni lives with. He's not her boyfriend or anything, so, technically speaking, we're not related, but he's lived with Joni for my whole life, and we consider each other family. Tom is an alcohol-and-drug counselor and does some night shifts at the Youth Detox, so he sleeps odd hours and half the time he's wandering around the house in his pajamas in the middle of the day.

"My dad's...This woman Dad has met," I said.

Tom rubbed his curly hair with one hand. "Ahh. Yes. Peter's new girlfriend." He crossed the kitchen, squeezed my shoulder with one hand and took a cookie from the tin with the other.

Girlfriend. It sounded so stupid.

He took a bite of cookie and closed his eyes. "Joni, Joni, Joni. You're killing me, you know." He chewed in silence for a moment; then he opened his eyes and looked at me. "So, Fiona. I take it you're not exactly excited about this budding relationship?" he asked.

"You could say that."

"Well, I'm hardly in a position to comment on other people's romances, given my own track record." He gave a long dramatic sigh, but he didn't really sound too sad.

Tom's had plenty of boyfriends, and they've all been smart and funny and nice, but it never seems to turn into anything long-term. Joni says that neither she nor Tom is the settling-down kind. Which is kind of funny in a way, because they act like an old married couple, and when they take me out, people always assume they're my grandparents. I don't mind, but Tom is always quick to point out that he's nearly eight years younger than Joni, and while she might be ready to look like a grandparent, he most certainly is not.

I pushed the cookie tin closer to Tom, hoping he'd take my side. "It's not that I don't want Dad to be happy, but Kathy is kind of weird. She says she's psychic."

Tom nodded. "Joni told me. You're not worried she'll be reading your mind or something? Looking in her crystal ball to find out what you and your friends are up too?"

I snorted. "Hardly."

"So what's the big deal?"

"I don't think they're right for each other," I said. "I think she's a liar and a fake, and I don't want Dad getting involved with her. She's a fraud."

Joni raised her eyebrows and leaned forward, elbows on the counter. "Does she actually take money from people? For…what do they call them? Readings?"

I nodded. "Yeah. That's what she does for a living."

Joni's eyebrows disappeared under her masses of wild gray curls. "Well, I hadn't realized that. I thought it was just a hobby."

I pursued my point. "So you see what I mean? It's not right, is it? Taking money and making things up like that?"

Joni hesitated. "We don't know exactly what she does."

"Yeah, but, okay, say we're not talking about anyone in particular. Say it's all—"

"Hypothetical," Tom said helpfully.

"Yeah. Say it's hypothetical. If someone—person A—was taking money from someone else—"

"Person B," Tom said.

I looked at him suspiciously, not sure if he was making fun of me. He took another cookie from the tin and grinned at me.

"Person B," I agreed. "And pretending to tell her future, say. Or giving her messages from her dead husband or whatever. Wouldn't that be, you know, wrong?"

"Unethical," Joni said, nodding firmly. "Yes."

I turned my hands palm up. "Well then. I rest my case."

Tom cocked his head to one side thoughtfully. "You're resting it on a pretty big assumption."

"What assumption?" I asked, frowning.

Tom glanced at Joni apologetically. "Well, we don't know that she's pretending."

Joni looked at him, eyebrows lifting. "You mean maybe she really believes she's psychic? I suppose that's possible."

I groaned. "Great. Dad could have a girlfriend who's crazy instead of one who is a liar. Thanks a lot, I feel so much better." I couldn't even say the word *girlfriend* without my voice changing, becoming hard and mocking and sarcastic.

"Actually," Tom said, "that's not what I meant."

Joni and I both stared at him. Don't say it, I thought. Please don't say it.

"Maybe she's the real thing," he said.

I clenched my hands into tight fists. Thinking about Kathy being able to communicate with Mom made my whole body ache. If anyone was going to communicate with my mother, it should be me. It definitely should not be some weird stranger who was after Dad.

"Tom!" Joni practically vibrated with anger. "Give your head a shake! That's the most ludicrous…the most absurd…the plain stupidest…"

"I'm just saying, hypothetically, we should consider all the possibilities."

"Right," she snapped. "The *possibilities*. Not the impossibilities. And the possibilities are that Kathy is either a liar or a fool. Not that she can talk to people who have died." She stopped abruptly and looked at me like she'd just remembered I was there. "Fiona, you're not thinking she can actually do that, are you?"

I swallowed hard and shook my head. "No one can."

"That's right." Joni's mouth tightened. "None of us can do that." She tugged on the beaded chain of her reading glasses, twisting it in her hand. There was a soft pop, and beads flew across the kitchen in a bright spray of blue and green and purple, pinging off the cupboards and rolling across the tiles. "Damn it, Tom! Look what you made me do."

Tom looked at me. "Sorry, kiddo. I didn't mean to upset you."

It seemed to me Joni was the one who was upset. "I'm fine," I told him.

Joni picked up a bead that was rolling across the countertop toward her. Her hand shook slightly. "Fiona. There's no need to mention what I said to your father. The part about Kathy being a liar or a fool. I shouldn't have said that."

"Don't worry, I won't tell on you." I stifled a giggle. "It's true though."

"Maybe it is, and maybe it isn't. If Peter is happy…" She shrugged her shawl-covered shoulders. "I should accept things as they are. We all should."

The urge to giggle dissolved and left my mouth tasting as dry and bitter as if I'd eaten a fistful of lemon peel. I couldn't accept Kathy, and I wasn't going to try.

"I miss Jennifer too, you know." Joni looked at me. "But life has to go on. Jennifer is gone, and your father is still here. He has to do what is best for him."

I looked away, unable to meet her eyes. I wondered if she knew that I had taken Mom's side—that I'd encouraged her to go on that last sailing trip.

"It'd be nice to see Peter happy," Joni said. "So just think about that, okay?"

If being happy meant forgetting about Mom, then I wasn't sure I wanted Dad to be happy. I wasn't sure I even wanted to be happy myself.

nine

After I went to bed that night, I couldn't stop thinking about what Tom had said. *Maybe she's the real thing.* I didn't believe it, but as long as there was the slightest possibility that Kathy could communicate with my mother—even a speck-sized possibility—it was going to be impossible for me to put the thought out of my head.

I got out of bed and rummaged through the laundry hamper until I found the dirty jeans I'd worn on the weekend. There it was, in the back pocket: Kathy's business card. It was white and fairly plain, with simple black lettering. *Katherine Morrison, Medium and Clairvoyant Empath.* Her phone number. A small, finely drawn figure of a young girl in the top corner. I tore it in half, dropped the pieces in the garbage and got back into bed.

It didn't help. My thoughts ran in endless, point-less, restless circles. What if, what if, what if…

I guess I eventually fell asleep, because when I woke up the next morning, my pillow was wet with tears and I'd had a horrible dream. I'd gone to the marina and *Eliza J* had been gone. Sold. I'd lain on the splintery wooden dock and cried and cried.

I sat up and wiped my eyes with my sleeve. Just a dream, I told myself. But it didn't help. It didn't take away the awful empty ache inside me. It didn't even touch it.

Besides, it wasn't just a dream. For all I knew, *Eliza J* really could be gone.

Dad was drinking coffee and reading the news-paper when I came downstairs. I made myself some toast and poured a glass of milk before joining him at the kitchen table. I ducked my head as I sat down, not wanting him to notice my puffy eyes, but I needn't have worried. He didn't even look up from his paper.

I couldn't help thinking that Mom would have noticed right away. She'd have given me a consid-ering look, like she wanted to ask if I was okay but didn't want to pry. And then she'd have asked anyway. She always did. Dad wasn't like that. I knew he loved me and everything, but he hadn't ever been the noticing type. And since Mom died, he noticed even less than ever.

I had to get to the marina before school. I needed to see *Eliza J*. I needed to make sure that she was still there. "I have to go in early," I told Dad between mouthfuls of toast and peanut butter.

He nodded without looking up.

"Aliens from Jupiter are coming to our homeroom class," I said.

He nodded again.

"So I may not come home, you know. I may go back to their planet with them."

Another nod.

I picked up my plate and put it into the dishwasher. My hands were shaking. If I stayed in the room with Dad for another second, I would throw something at him.

Eliza J was still there. The For Sale sign was still there too. I stepped aboard and sat in the cockpit, looking around the marina. Most of the people who had boats here were men, and most were Dad's age or older. I didn't know any other girls who were into sailing. It was sort of discouraging, but all the same, when Mom was here, I never doubted that I'd be a sailor. She'd given me a book for my tenth birthday about a girl called Tania Aebi, who'd sailed around the world on her own, starting when she was eighteen. That had been my dream ever since: to circumnavigate the globe right after high school.

I let my hand rest on the tiller, closed my eyes and imagined being out at sea, me and my boat alone under a starry sky. I imagined the sound of waves breaking, the feel of the wind on my face, the taste of salt spray on my lips. Trade winds, flying fish, sunsets and dolphins. Just me and my boat, all the way to Hawaii, Fiji, Tonga, New Zealand. I had always been so sure I'd do it someday.

Now I didn't feel sure of anything.

"I went to the library last night," Abby told me at lunch the next day. "I got a ton of books for our project."

We were sitting on the bleachers by the football field, and the midday sun was warm in that distant sort of way that makes you lift your face toward it and long for summer. "Great. Did you figure out how we can prove Kathy is a fake?"

"Well, we'll have to be kind of subtle." She looked at me doubtfully. "Not too obvious."

"I know what subtle means, thanks."

"Yeah. Um, it's just that you tend to be pretty direct. I mean, that's a good thing, Fi. But for this…"

"Okay, okay. I get it."

"Good. So do you want to get together after school and go over stuff?"

I nodded. "Sure. But I'm going to Joni's." I didn't think Joni would mind if Abby came with me, but Dad was pretty firm about telling me not to take advantage of Joni's generosity by inviting friends over there. "Do you think you could come over later? Like for dinner?"

Abby shrugged. "I'll ask. Probably. Hey, can I sleep over?"

"Yes! Well, I'll check, but that'd be great."

"We could get a lot done. Figure this project out and get a good start on it."

Usually the thought of spending a Friday evening on homework would make my heart sink, but not this time. I couldn't wait to get to work on getting rid of Kathy. She didn't know it yet, but she was history. "I guess if she was really psychic, she'd know what we were doing," I said aloud.

Abby looked puzzled. "Who would? What are you talking about?"

"Kathy. If she was psychic, she'd be getting nervous, don't you think?"

Abby shrugged. "If she was psychic, she'd have nothing to be nervous about."

"I guess." The green paint was peeling on the metal benches of the bleachers, and I picked at it with my fingernail.

Abby winced. "Stop it. That noise makes my skin crawl."

I stopped and folded my hands together. "Anyway, she isn't psychic. No one is. But she should be nervous. Because we're going to figure out a way to get rid of her." I tried to grin.

"Fiona…"

"Goodbye, Kathy," I said. My voice sounded fiercer than I intended it to. I meant it though. I didn't care how great Dad said she was. I wanted her out of our lives.

Joni was painting her kitchen, talking on the phone and making cookies, all at the same time. I nibbled at the cookies cooling on the counter and read a magazine. Finally, she put the phone down, winked at me, pulled a tray of cookies out of the oven and stripped off a giant cooking apron decorated with Christmas elves and splattered with yellow paint.

"Multitasking prevents Alzheimer's," she told me. "Or so I hope. You look like you had a better day today."

"I did." I opened my mouth to tell her about the plans Abby and I were making, but quickly closed it again. I was pretty sure Joni wouldn't approve.

Besides, we hadn't figured out how we were going to do it yet.

The phone rang.

Joni picked it up. "Hello…uh-huh…uh-huh… okay, I'll tell her…okay, we'll see you soon."

She hung up and turned to me. "Your dad. He says he'll be here in a few minutes to pick you up on his way home."

"He's early," I protested. "And I have my bike. I was going to stop at the marina."

"He says Kathy and Caitlin are coming for dinner, so he's leaving work early." Joni looked at the half-empty cookie tray. "You're not going to have much appetite."

"Seriously?" I stared at her. "We just had dinner with them. Like, two nights ago."

"Mmm."

I slipped down from my stool and leaned against the counter. "This is so not fair, Joni. Just because Dad wants to…wants to…"

She gave me a sympathetic smile. "Give it a chance."

"I hate her." My throat was suddenly tight, and I had to stop talking or I'd start bawling. I turned away and stood there with my back to Joni.

"Oh, honey." She stood there behind me, not quite touching. I could hear her breathing. I could feel her wanting to touch me and not knowing if she should. If she did, I thought I might fall apart completely.

I sniffed and wiped the back of my hand across my eyes. It wasn't fair. I took a deep breath and blinked away my tears. Tom walked into the room with a grin and a wink.

"Hey there, chickie. What's up?"

"Not much." I blew out a long breath and made a face. "Apparently, I have to have dinner with dad's flaky lying psychic girlfriend."

His eyebrows shot up. "Do I detect a note of displeasure?"

"You could say that."

Tom nodded. "Yeah. Well, it's gotta be tough. No matter what she was like, I don't imagine you'd be thrilled about your dad dating yet."

"Exactly. Because it's too soon. It is, right?" I looked up at him hopefully. "It's only been a year. He shouldn't be getting involved with anyone."

Tom and Joni exchanged glances.

"Right? He shouldn't. Especially…you know, someone who tells lies and pretends she knows what's going to happen next. Because that's bull. It's bull. No one knows what's going to happen." My breath caught in my throat.

Tom pulled me in for a crushing bear hug. "Hang in there, chickie. You'll get through this."

There was a honk outside. I looked out the window and saw Dad's car pulling up in the driveway. I pulled away from Tom and looked up at his face. "You don't think she could actually be psychic, do you?"

He glanced at Joni, shrugged and spread his arms out wide. "World's a big, strange place."

I frowned at him, frustrated. "Yeah, but, come on, Tom. You know she has to be a fake."

"Most people spend their lives looking for some kind of certainty." Tom ruffled my hair. "Me, I tend to see certainty as a state of mind best avoided."

"Okay. Fine. But talking to dead people?"

Joni snorted, and Tom shook his head. Without anyone saying a word, I knew we were all thinking about Mom.

Dad honked again.

"I guess we're in a hurry," I said flatly.

Joni gave me a quick pat on the shoulder. Tom wrapped his arms around me, his beard tickling my cheek.

"You hang in there, kiddo," he told me again.

ten

"How come you didn't come in to say hi?" I asked Dad as I got in the car.

"Put your seat belt on."

"I am. Jeez." I buckled up, watching him. He was frowning. "Is everything okay?"

"Fine." He backed up without checking the rearview mirror and slammed the brakes on. "Damn cyclists."

I looked over my shoulder. A teenage girl on a bicycle flipped Dad off. "Well, she did have the right of way. You weren't looking."

He ignored my comment, pulled out of the driveway more carefully and started driving toward home. "We're picking up Chinese. I phoned in an order," he said after a minute.

"Whatever. How come we have to see them again? We just saw them on Tuesday."

"Fiona, don't start." He sounded weary, like I was such a pain in the backside.

"I'm not starting anything," I said, stung. "I was just asking."

"I'm seeing quite a bit of Kathy," he said after a pause. "I know that's upsetting for you, and I can understand that, but I think it'll help if you get to know her. Honestly, Fiona, I think you'd like her if you gave her a chance. If you tried to see her as a real person, not just…"

"Some phony who pretends to be able to talk to dead people?"

He tightened his hands on the wheel and gave me a level glance. "Not as someone who's trying to take your mother's place."

"She can't do that."

"No. She knows she can't. She doesn't want to. But if you'd let her, I think she could be a good friend."

"Yeah, right." I rolled my eyes.

Dad shook his head like he was disappointed in me, and neither of us said anything more. There didn't seem to be much to say. When Dad ran into Jade Garden to pick up the sweet-and-sour chicken, honey-garlic spareribs and pork fried rice, I closed my eyes and tried to picture Mom's face. I couldn't do it. I could picture the photos I had of her, but I couldn't actually see her real face in my mind. It kept slipping away.

*
* *
* *

I guess Dad must have given Kathy a key, because when we got home, she and Caitlin were already inside, setting our dining-room table and getting drinks out of our refrigerator. It was totally weird. Dad and I never even used the dining room. I stood around feeling like this wasn't my house at all.

"Sit, sit!" Kathy invited us to the table like she was the one who lived here. Dad sat down, grinning like everything was just wonderful. I ignored him and took the seat beside Caitlin, who kept staring at me, her straight blond hair hanging limply around her pale little face. I felt like throwing something at her, but instead I just asked her to pass the spareribs. Despite Joni's cookies, I was starving.

Kathy helped herself to some sweet-and-sour chicken. "This is delicious." Red goop dropped from her fork and splattered Mom's favorite tablecloth, a white one embroidered with tiny flowers. She wiped at it with her napkin, making a big ugly smear. "I'm taking Caitlin shopping tomorrow. She's outgrown all her clothes from last year. We're just going to the mall, but I wondered if you might like to come along."

"Me? Why?" I couldn't think of anything I wanted less.

"For fun. You must need something, don't you? Capris? A new dress? Summer's coming up." She laughed. "That's our excuse, at least."

If she was psychic, she'd have known I didn't wear dresses. Actually, if she was even mildly observant, she'd have known. "Thanks, but I'll pass."

"I think it's a great idea," Dad said. "I can't even remember the last time you got new clothes."

No doubt. Buying me clothes had been Mom's job. Sometimes Joni picked up a new hoodie or pair of jeans for me. Dad never even seemed to notice.

"I hate shopping," I said.

"There's no need to be rude about it." He looked a little taken aback. He took his glasses off and rubbed them on his shirt. Without his wire rims framing his eyes, he looked kind of exposed and vulnerable, like a crab without its shell.

"Think about it," Kathy said lightly. "You don't have to decide right now."

I slid the chow mein toward my plate and dished myself a large scoop of noodles. "Actually, I'm busy tomorrow. I have plans with Abby."

"What are you doing?" Caitlin asked quickly.

I wondered if she had guessed I was lying about having plans. "It's not really any of your business," I told her. My voice was sharper than I meant it to be.

Dad put his glasses back on and instantly was his usual, slightly grouchy self again. "Fiona! That is enough. You are being inexcusably rude."

I pushed my plate away, suddenly not hungry. "Whatever." I snuck a sideways glance at Caitlin, who was still staring at me. Her expression hadn't changed, but her cheeks were turning pink.

"Excuse us a moment," Dad said. He grabbed my arm, hustled me into the hallway and closed the door.

I pulled my arm free and stared back at him, my stomach a tight ball of anger.

I thought he was going to yell at me, but he didn't say anything at all for a long time. Finally he sighed, his hands hanging limp at his sides. "Fiona. That was beyond rude. It was unkind. I'm ashamed of you." His frown carved deep creases between his eyes. "I know this is hard for you, okay? You've made that pretty obvious. And I am trying to be understanding, but enough is enough. Caitlin's just a kid. She's had plenty to deal with herself, but she's managing to be friendly and polite. I don't see you even making an effort."

I glared at him. "None of this was my idea. I don't want her here. I don't want Kathy here. And if you woke up and saw that she's a fraud, maybe you wouldn't want her here either."

He stepped back abruptly. "This conversation is over," he said. "My relationship with Kathy is not up for discussion."

"But Dad—"

"To your room. Now."

I slammed the door behind me, cut through the kitchen and grabbed two apples from the fridge drawer. Then I went up to my room, threw myself on the bed and ate them while staring at the ceiling. There were about a thousand cracks on it. I usually liked making pictures out of them—seeing faces, or sailboats, or animals.

Tonight, all those cracks just made me feel like everything was falling apart.

eleven

A few minutes later there was a knock at my door. "What?"

The door opened a crack, and Caitlin poked her head in.

"What do you want?" I said rudely.

"Mom said I should come up and hang out with you, but you don't have to talk to me if you don't want to." Caitlin's voice was so quiet I could hardly hear her, and she looked a bit scared: all wide-eyed like some baby animal. I thought it was kind of mean of Kathy to send her up here just so she and Dad could be alone together.

"You can come in," I said awkwardly. "It's nothing personal, you know. I just don't think my dad should be seeing so much of your mother."

She shrugged and slipped through my door, closing it behind her. "I know. I don't want them dating either."

"You don't?"

Caitlin tucked a limp strand of blond hair behind her ear. Everything about her was pale: almost white hair, skin that looked like it had never seen the sun, transparent blue eyes. She looked like one of those albino bunny rabbits.

She shook her head. "No offence, but your Dad's all wrong for my Mom. He's too old, for a start."

"He's not old."

Caitlin shrugged again. "Whatever."

My thoughts were racing. Even though I agreed with her that Dad and Kathy were wrong for each other, I didn't like her comment about Dad being old. Not that I disagreed—I'd said pretty much the same thing the other night when I pointed out the age difference between him and Kathy. I just wouldn't have expected Caitlin to be so direct.

On the other hand, if she didn't want them together either, maybe she could help me figure out a way to put a stop to it. I narrowed my eyes, wondering how much to trust her. "So your Mom's a psychic. Like, professionally?"

"Yeah. That's another reason I don't think she should be involved with your Dad." She rolled her pale eyes with what looked like scorn. "He's got no spiritual abilities at all."

I could feel my jaw drop. "Excuse me? You don't think she should date my dad because he's *not* a psychic? That's, like, the dumbest thing I've ever heard."

"Sorry." Her cheeks went instantly pink.

"Seriously. You can't actually believe the whole psychic thing?"

Caitlin looked at me straight on. "Mom's not a fake, if that's what you're thinking. She's helped a lot of people."

"Yeah, I'll bet." Helped them to hand over their money, I thought. "You're in grade six, right? I guess you'll be going to middle school next year?"

"I homeschool," Caitlin said. She looked around my room. "What's with all the maps?"

"Those aren't maps," I said. "They're charts."

My walls are covered with nautical charts. They're old and out of date, but I didn't mind. It's not as if the oceans change that much from year to year. Though I guessed they might, if global warming continued. I pushed that thought away, because thinking about climate change always made me anxious. I stood and crossed the room to stand beside Caitlin. "South Pacific," I said. "The little brown dots are islands. Lots of them are uninhabited."

Caitlin screwed up her pale little face. "Who'd want to go to an island no one lives on? There'd be nothing there."

I looked at her incredulously. "Yeah. That'd be the point. Duh."

A hint of pink rose in her cheeks.

"You could go somewhere else," I said quickly. "That's the whole thing about sailing; that's why it's so great. You could sail to San Francisco or New York. Europe. Africa. Australia. Anywhere you want."

Caitlin looked unimpressed. "You could fly to any of those places in a lot less time."

"Yeah, sure, but sailing…"

"I took some lessons last summer," Caitlin said. "It was kind of boring."

All the air rushed out of my lungs in a big *whoosh.* I couldn't stand it.

"Well," I said, "it's been nice chatting with you, but I have homework to do."

Caitlin just stood there looking dumb, so I grabbed my books and pushed past her, out the door and downstairs to the kitchen. Dad and Kathy were in the living room, talking. Their voices drifted in, but I couldn't hear what they were saying. I picked up the phone and speed-dialed Abby.

"You have to rescue me," I said. "This is a nightmare."

"Hold on," she said. Then she yelled "Mom!" without taking the phone away from her mouth, practically rupturing my eardrum.

I held the phone several inches away from my ear and listened to Abby telling her mom that we absolutely had to start work on our science project right away. Muffled response.

"Fiona?"

I put the phone back to my ear gingerly. "Yeah?"

"Mom says you can come over here or I can come to your house. To work on our science project. I can sleep over, she says."

I hesitated. What I wanted was to get out of my house, but Dad was more likely to agree to Abby coming over. Or not. He was pretty mad at me. "I'll go check with Dad," I said slowly, "but if you came over here, you could talk to Kathy. Maybe you could help me figure out a way to prove that she's a fake."

*
* *
* *

Dad wasn't crazy about the idea of Abby coming over.

"It's almost seven," he said.

"It's a Friday," I countered.

"And we have company. Do you really need to get started on this assignment tonight?"

"Absolutely." I held my breath.

"Caitlin can watch a movie with us," Kathy said quickly.

Dad took his glasses off and rubbed his hands over his face. "Abby's mom says she can sleep over?"

I nodded.

"All right. All right." He replaced his glasses on his nose and looked at me sternly through them. "But I expect you two to be working. And going to bed at a reasonable hour. Got it?"

"Got it!"

I dashed back to the phone and told Abby that she'd better bring a good-sized stack of books.

Caitlin, Kathy and Dad were watching some sappy movie when Abby arrived. Caitlin's choice, I'd bet. She looked like the sappy-movie type. I pushed Abby into the den ahead of me and introduced her.

Kathy lifted the remote control from the arm of the couch and paused the movie. On-screen, a group of girls froze in mid-giggle.

"It is very nice to meet you," Abby said. She was using the voice she uses when she talks to adults, which is different than her regular voice. She enunciates all her words carefully so that she sounds almost British.

Kathy smiled at her. "You too, Abby." You'd never have guessed they'd met before.

Caitlin turned her head slightly and nodded, but her eyes kept flicking back to the screen.

Abby looked at me. "I guess we'd better get to work," she said. She lifted an enormous bag of books to make her point. "We have a lot to do."

*
· * ·
* *

Up in my room, I made a face at her. "Well. That was brief. I thought you were going to help me prove she's fake."

Abby dumped the books on my bed with unnecessary force. "What did you expect me to say? 'Hi, nice to see you again, you big liar'?"

"No." I sighed. "I don't know how we're going to be able to prove anything."

"Don't despair," Abby said. "While you've been eating Chinese food and freaking out, I've been doing some research." She gestured at the books spilling across my bed. "At the library."

I picked up the book on the top of the pile and read out loud: "*Pyschic Phenomena: A Beginner's Guide to the Paranormal.*"

Abby nodded. "I figured we'd need to understand the basics. Learn the language, you know? So that we know what it is she does and what to look for."

"*Mediums and Messages*," I read. I put it aside and picked up another one. "*Psychics: Scams and Schemes*. That sounds good." I looked at the next book in the stack and laughed out loud. "*Be Your Own Psychic*. Ha. Maybe I could read my own mind."

Abby tossed a book at me. A heavy one. "Ouch." I glanced at the cover. "*The Idiot's Guide to Extrasensory Perception*? Are you trying to tell me something?"

There was a knock on the door.

I covered the book with my sweatshirt sleeve. "Yes?"

Dad poked his head in. "Just checking that all's well."

"Everything's fine," I said shortly.

I waited until the door had closed again before turning to Abby. "Phew. Just checking that we're doing our homework, more likely."

"Well, we are."

I'd been so focused on proving that Kathy was a fake, I'd forgotten that this was also supposed to be our science project.

* * *

By ten thirty, we were sitting amid a pile of books, paper, Coke cans and pretzel crumbs. I was exhausted, but we had an outline for our science project. I read it out loud:

Problem: How do psychics know things that logically they couldn't know?

Hypothesis: We believe that various forms of trickery are being used by these so-called mediums and psychics who claim to be communicating with the dead. We believe that psychic phenomena such as precognition (seeing the future) do not exist, and we intend to demonstrate this.

Method:
   1.   We will observe a psychic at work. We will be alert for evidence of trickery, and we will record our observations.
   2.   We will use a deck of cards and see if our test subjects can predict—more often than would be explained by chance—which card will be turned over next. This will test for precognition or knowing the future.
   3.   We will use the same deck of cards to test for telepathy, or mind-reading. One person will look at a card and attempt to "send" the image to the test subject. We will see if the subject's guesses reveal a higher level of success than expected by chance.

I made a face. "It's going to be a lot of work. And Kathy might not even agree to be a test subject."

"Yeah." She studied our notes. "Kathy's a medium, right? As well as a psychic."

"She's a liar."

"You know what I mean." Abby touched her lower lip thoughtfully. "Do you think we should try to, you know, communicate with someone dead as well? Like, be open to it and maybe see if anything happens?"

I stared at her.

Abby's cheeks turned pink. "I didn't mean…"

"If it was possible…" My voice shook. I took a deep breath and started over. "If it was possible, don't you think my mom would have done it by now? Don't you think if it was as easy as that, she'd send me messages too?"

Abby hesitated.

"What?" I could feel that tight shaky feeling starting up in my chest again, the roaring noise in my ears like the sound of waves in a shell. I forced myself to take another long breath. I hadn't ever lost it in front of Abby, and I didn't want to start now.

"Look, don't get mad," she said.

"Don't say anything stupid and I won't get mad."

She blew out an exasperated breath. "It's just a thought. Actually, forget it."

"What?"

She shook her head. "No big deal."

I wanted to shake her. "Okay, *okay*. I promise I won't get mad."

"Well, I wondered if maybe you haven't been open to it because, you know, you don't think it's possible. And maybe—probably not, but we can't rule it out—people who really believe in it and are open to it can see or hear things that the rest of us can't."

"I don't believe it," I said. "I think once you're dead, you're dead. And that's that." I couldn't help wondering though. *I feel as if there is someone who has a message for you,* Kathy had said the first time she met me. What if my mother really was out there somewhere? What if she was trying to tell me something and I just wasn't listening?

There was a knock at the door. Dad's face poked through the crack. "Girls? Don't tell me you're still up."

"Just getting in bed now," I told him. We turned off the lights and snuggled down, Abby on an air mattress on the floor and me in my bed. Within minutes, I heard Abby's breathing shift to the soft, even rhythm of sleep, while I lay awake staring into the darkness and trying to remember the sound of my mother's steps on the stairs.

twelve

We were woken by a loud knocking at my bedroom door.

I opened my eyes. "Mmph?" It felt awfully early, but bright sunlight was streaming in through a crack between the curtains.

The door opened, and Dad's head poked in. "Fiona? Kathy just called to see if you wanted to go shopping with them after all."

I groaned. "No. I told her already."

"Fine." Dad cleared his throat. "Come on downstairs. I'm making waffles, and Abby's mom is picking her up in half an hour."

Abby pulled the covers off her head. "We'll be right down."

He gave her a grateful smile before retreating.

As soon as the door closed, I scowled at her. "Traitor. All you care about is the waffles."

"How come you never told me she invited you to go shopping with them? You totally have to go." Abby clambered awkwardly off the air mattress and grabbed her clothes from the pile on the floor. "It's a great opportunity to ask her some questions without your dad around."

I flopped back down on my bed. "Ugh. You make it sound so easy."

"Tell her about our science project," Abby suggested. She balled up my blue jeans and tossed them at me. "Or ask her about her work."

I caught the jeans without sitting up. "I'm not going, Abby."

"Fiona, come on. How are you going to prove she's fake if you don't take these opportunities to investigate?"

"Easy for you to say. Besides, it's too late. I already said no."

"So tell your dad you changed your mind. He'll probably be happy."

I pulled my jeans on. "Don't you think it's weird, the way Dad wants me to get to know her? I mean, so he's dating or whatever. But why involve me? Why do I have to get to know her? Unless…" I broke off, not wanting to finish the thought out loud.

Abby shook her head. "It's too soon. They've only been seeing each other for a few months."

"He gave her a key to our house," I whispered.

"Don't go there. Seriously, Fi."

I stared at her mutely. I didn't want to go there. But I was getting this awful feeling that Dad might.

"In any case, if you're right—if they are getting serious—that's all the more reason to go shopping with her. To get some information. Knowledge is power, right?" Abby tilted her head to one side, eyebrows raised. "You might not have much time to waste."

*   *
*   *

Down in the kitchen, Dad was whistling. I have to admit he makes the best waffles. He makes them from scratch, different every time. This morning's were made with buttermilk and blueberries, and doused with maple syrup. He piled them on our plates and waited. He's like a little kid when he does this: hanging around to see what we think, wanting to hear how good they are. Abby had been eating his waffles for years, and he knew he could always count on her for a favorable review.

She took a big bite, closed her eyes and moaned. "Mmmm," she said, "these are out of this world."

Dad grinned. "You like?"

"I *love.*"

I grudgingly ate a few bites, trying to ignore Dad, who was lingering in the doorway.

They really were good.

"Okay," I finally said, exasperated. "This combo's a keeper."

Dad winked at me. "That's my girl." He wandered off to the living room, whistling to himself.

Abby put down her fork. "Fi?"

"Yeah."

"Don't get mad, but your dad seems so happy."

"I know." The waffle turned to soggy cardboard in my mouth. I willed Abby not to say aloud what I knew we were both thinking.

"Maybe we shouldn't interfere," she said, staring at her plate. Clearly, she wasn't telepathic. "You know?" She glanced up at me. "If they're happy…if your dad's happy…"

"It's not just about them, Abby. This is my life too, and I'm not going to let Dad wreck it because he's having some midlife crisis." I pushed my plate away. "Kathy's either a loony who thinks she's talking to dead people, or she's a fraud who's deliberately ripping people off. Either way, believe me, Dad's better off without her." Under the table, my hands curled into tight fists. Abby was right. Knowledge was power, and I might not have any time to waste.

"Dad!" I called. "Can I change my mind about going shopping? I just remembered that I really need new jeans."

* * *

Outside, the air was cool and fresh, the sky a soft damp gray. I looked longingly at my bicycle, chained to the front porch railing, and wished I was going down to the marina or over to Joni's place or still sitting in the kitchen eating waffles and waiting for Abby's mom to pick her up. Anything but this.

Kathy jumped out of her car and opened the back door for me. "Thanks for coming," she said. "I was so glad when your dad said you'd changed your mind."

She wouldn't be so glad if she knew why. I slipped into the car behind Caitlin, who was wearing a short white skirt and a fluffy pink sweater. The car was spotless and smelled new, like leather and shampoo. I thought of our old Toyota and the way it always had empty pop cans and potato-chip bags scrunched under the seats.

I buckled my seat belt, avoiding her eyes, and we drove in silence for a while. I was trying to think of ways to ask Kathy about her work without being too obvious.

She drove fast, moving into the passing lane and skimming along Douglas Street toward the mall. The engine purred quietly, and some classical music played softly on the stereo. Dad never speeds, but that may be because our car starts to rattle before we even get close to the speed limit.

I hate you, Kathy, I thought. I watched her face in the rearview mirror. If she could read my mind, she wasn't showing any signs of it. I tried thinking loudly, projecting my thoughts toward her like arrows. Stones. Missiles. *I hate you, and I'm not going to let you be with my dad.* The car purred along, smooth and quiet, and Kathy didn't say a word.

"So," I said, "I was wondering how you became a medium."

There was a pause. Caitlin glanced over her shoulder at me.

Kathy's hands tapped the steering wheel. Nervously, I thought. Didn't that suggest she was hiding something?

"It's a long story," she said. "Are you sure you want to hear it?"

"I'm really interested," I told her, trying to inject some sincerity into my voice.

Caitlin turned and glanced at me again, but said nothing. When she turned away, she thumped back against her seat, stiff-shouldered. I wondered what that was about, but kept my eyes on the half of Kathy's face that I could see in the rearview mirror.

"I had another child, before Caitlin," Kathy said.

"You *did*?" I wondered why Dad hadn't told me that.

Caitlin turned on the radio. Country station.

"Caitlin, do you mind? We're talking." Kathy snapped it off again, sounding annoyed. "She was born the year after Jack and I got married. Her name was Nicole."

Was. Did that mean what I thought it did? Kathy paused as if she was waiting for me to ask, but I didn't say anything. I was not going to feel sorry for Kathy, even if she told me she had a dozen dead kids. She couldn't suck me in that easily.

Kathy turned and looked at me. "I wanted to have lots of babies. But…well, after Nicole, I couldn't seem to get pregnant again. The doctors never found a reason. It was five years before Caitlin was born."

"The light's green," Caitlin said. The car behind us honked its horn.

Kathy stepped on the gas, and we accelerated abruptly. Caitlin opened her window and stuck one arm out, palm facing the wind.

"Anyway." Kathy looked up at the rearview mirror, and I accidentally met her eyes for a second. I dropped my eyes back to my lap quickly. "Three years ago, Jack and the girls were in a car accident.

They were on their way to a soccer game. Nicole's team was in the playoffs. Jack was driving. It wasn't his fault; the other driver was drunk. He plowed into them. Ran right through a red light."

My throat tightened. "Oh. That's awful."

"Yes. Jack was killed instantly. Nicole died in hospital a few days later. She was only a couple of months older than you are now—a few days away from her fourteenth birthday. And Caitlin was almost uninjured. Everyone said it was a miracle."

Some miracle, I thought. A dead husband and a dead kid. You'd think if someone was there that day and in the business of performing miracles, they could have been a bit more inclusive.

"And it was after that you became a medium?"

Kathy turned to look at me, which was a bit worrying, as we were speeding along a busy road and talking about car accidents. "I couldn't imagine how I could keep going. Only I had to, of course, for Caitlin."

Caitlin's face was turned away so I couldn't see her expression. She would have been eight or nine when her dad and her sister died, I calculated, and I felt a sharp stab of shame about how mean I had been to her.

Kathy looked back at the road. "I don't know if this makes sense to you or not, but I felt so guilty."

I swallowed. I knew all about guilt, but I couldn't let myself think about that, or the whirlpool would suck me right in.

"I should have been with them that day, going to the game, but I had the flu." Her hands were gripping the wheel so tightly her knuckles were white. "I kept thinking that if I had been there, maybe I could have done something. After Jack and Nicole died, I was so depressed I could hardly get out of bed."

Like Dad, I thought, remembering all those weeks I stayed with Joni and Tom.

"Then one day, I saw a poster inviting everyone to a meeting at a spiritualist church. I remember exactly what it said: *Lost someone you love? Seeking comfort?* I'd never been very religious. I'd never given much thought to what happens after we die, to be honest. But when I saw this poster, I thought, Well, why not? What do I have to lose?"

"And what happened?" I asked.

"I know this might be hard to believe, but I received a message," she said. "A message from beyond. From Jack, that first time, telling me that he and Nicole were together and that everything was okay."

"Huh. How did you receive it? Could you, like, hear his voice?"

Kathy shook her head. "One of mediums at the church meeting—a wonderful man—he picked me out of the crowd and said he had a message for me. He asked if he could come to me, and I said yes, and he came over and told me that he could see a tall man— Jack was very tall—and that the man wanted to tell me that he loved me."

I nodded, caught up in the story despite myself. "And?"

"And then the medium said, 'You have lost someone else too.' And I started crying and told him about Nicole. 'Yes,' he said. 'She was so young.' Just like he could see her."

I thought again about Abby's words: *it's all acting and guesswork.* It wasn't a huge leap for someone to guess that Kathy's daughter would have been young.

"After that I went to meetings for a while. And then I started getting messages myself. Directly. From Nicole, mostly." Kathy took one hand off the steering wheel and rested it on Caitlin's knee. "It was incredible, just incredible, to speak to her again. I thought she was lost forever, but she turned out to be so close."

I thought she was lost forever. All I could think about was Mom. *She turned out to be so close.* I blinked back tears so hot, they were scalding my eyes. Get a grip, I told myself. Only idiots believe this stuff.

I cleared my throat. "So, do you talk to them both? Your daughter and your…" I wanted to say ex-husband, but that made it sound like they were divorced.

"Jack never speaks to me directly," Kathy said sadly. "Though of course I have friends, other mediums, who pass on messages from him."

Like they were all on some kind of online social networking site. Twitter for dead people. "So do you, like, talk to them too?" I asked Caitlin.

She shook her head. "Mom gives me messages from them though."

Kathy squeezed her daughter's knee and, without slowing down, swung the steering wheel around with one hand as we turned into the mall's parking lot. I was starting to feel carsick.

"Caitlin is a bit sad about not having my abilities," Kathy said. "I tell her she shouldn't worry about it. It's a mixed blessing, you know?"

I cleared my throat. "If you say so."

Kathy pulled into a parking space, unbuckled her seat belt and turned to look at me over her shoulder. Rain was spattering lightly on the windshield. "It's a big responsibility. When I started receiving messages for other people, I didn't understand why I had been given this gift, but I felt I had no choice but to use it to help others." She met my eyes and gave a sudden, unexpected laugh. "If your eyes get any wider, they'll fall right out. But I don't blame you for being skeptical. If someone had told me a few years ago that I'd end up doing this, I'd have laughed my head off."

"But now you really believe it's possible that after someone has died…?"

"I know it is. I know that the spirits of those who have passed are still with us, and that they have a great deal of wisdom and comfort to share with us, if we only allow it." Kathy stopped abruptly. "And I know I'm talking way too much about myself and what I think." She waved her hands in the direction of the mall entrance. "Come on, girls. Let's go shopping."

"Ooh, can we go in there?" Caitlin asked as we walked through the doors. She pointed to a store window display.

I followed her gaze and tried not to shudder. Mannequins dressed in strapless ruffled dresses; racks and racks of outfits in pastel peach, baby blue, mint green, candy pink. It looked like Easter had exploded.

"Me and Mom love that store," Caitlin told me.

Me and Mom. My breath turned to ice in my lungs. *Me and Mom.* I'd give anything to be able to say those words again.

thirteen

Abby had to go to church on Sunday, but afterward her mom dropped her off at Joni and Tom's. I was already there, finishing off the deck of cards we'd made for our experiment. Five different cards, each with a different shape drawn on it in thick black marker.

Joni's kitchen was warm and filled with cooking smells: onions, garlic, curry spices. I tossed the cards on the kitchen table, and Abby and I pulled up chairs. Joni was sitting across from us, wearing an old stretched-out sweater. She pushed her hair back from her face and looked at us expectantly.

"Okay, Joni," I said. "This is the test for telepathy. I'll look at a card and concentrate on the shape. I'll try to project the image toward you. Take as long as you need before guessing."

Abby leaned forward and planted her elbows on the kitchen table. "Not guessing, Fi. She's supposed to wait until an image forms in her mind and then tell us which shape she sees."

I frowned. "Same diff."

"No, it's not. Guessing implies she's thinking about it. We don't want her to think, we want her to intuit."

"Intuit? Is that a word?"

Abby shrugged. "Use her intuition. Whatever."

"Okay. Okay. I think I have the general idea," Joni said.

Abby and I stopped arguing and looked across the table at her.

"Right," I said. "Ready?"

"Whenever you are."

I looked at the black circle on the first card, closed my eyes and tried to hold the image in my mind. "Okay. Take your time."

"Circle," Joni said.

My eyes flew open and I flipped the card around to face Joni. "That's incredible."

Abby grabbed the cards. "You're not supposed to tell her how she did until the end of the test, remember? She has to do ten cards. And even by chance, you'd expect her to get a couple right."

"Fine," I said. "You try."

She flipped a card up, hand cupped over it so Joni couldn't see. Triangle.

Joni closed her eyes for a moment. "Square."

Abby gave me a smug look. "See? Coincidence."

"Maybe," I said. "Or maybe you don't project the image as clearly as I do."

"Yeah, right. Anyway, since when do you believe in this?"

I scowled. "I don't."

Joni cleared her throat. "Could we get on with this? I actually have about a thousand things to do this afternoon."

"Sorry," Abby said quickly. "Ready for another?"

* * *

Joni got two right out of ten. A perfect score: 20 percent. Exactly what you'd expect by chance.

Abby and I had already tested each other several times. The test for precognition was much the same: the subject had to predict which card would be turned up next. I'd done a little better on that one than Abby had. I'd scored one out of ten, and she'd got zero. The telepathy test hadn't been much better: I got two right, same as Joni, and Abby got three. So far, no evidence of psychic powers. Big surprise.

Tom wandered into the kitchen, opened the fridge and frowned at the shelves. He grabbed a bag of baby carrots and plopped down on a chair beside us.

"Rabbit food, anyone?" he asked glumly.

I took a carrot. "Dieting?"

Tom nodded and patted his belly. "Yup. What else is new?"

"You look great," Abby said loyally.

He tilted his head to one side and smiled fondly at her. "Thanks, sugar."

"Can we test you, Tom?" I asked.

"This is for your science project, right?" Tom pulled a carrot out of the bag and inspected it closely. "Sure, I'll be your guinea pig."

"Don't worry, we're not allowed to kill or dissect anything," Abby said.

Tom laughed. "Well, that *is* a relief."

Abby explained the experiment as I got the cards ready.

"Telepathy first," I said. "I'm looking at the first card and visualizing the image. When you're ready, tell me what comes into your mind."

"Square," he said immediately. "Am I right?"

I shook my head. "Nope. Wavy lines. Oops." I shot a guilty glance at Abby. "I wasn't supposed to tell you that."

Tom sighed. "Well, I better not give up my day job yet."

By the end of the week, we had done the tests on half our classmates, Abby's mom, Joni and Tom, and each other. Nineteen subjects. We needed twenty to fit our original goal, and I knew who the last one had to be.

"I can't ask her," I said. "It's going to be so obvious."

It was lunchtime, and we were sitting on the school steps, watching a bunch of kids goofing around. A Frisbee came flying toward us, and Abby caught it neatly and tossed it back in one smooth motion. "Only if you make it obvious," she said, sitting back down. "What were you planning?" She mimicked my voice. "Hey, Kathy, can we do this test on you to see if you're a big fake?"

I made a face. "No, but I just feel like she'll guess we're up to something."

"Thought you didn't care what she thought."

"I don't. Dad'll freak out though."

"You want me to ask?"

I looked at her gratefully. "Would you?"

"Sure. Hey, I was thinking. The whole psychic thing. Don't you think it's sort of dramatic? You know, sort of attention-seeking? Because I was wondering if Kathy might have a personality disorder." She pulled a massive battered book out of the oversized backpack she always carried.

I grabbed the book. "What is this?"

"*The DSM*," Abby replied. "*The Diagnostic and Statistics Manual.* Psychiatrists and psychologists use it."

The book weighed about five pounds. I flipped some pages, reading quickly. "Jeez. Listen to this: 'If you have a feeling that the external world is strange, you could have derealization disorder.' That's stupid. What if the external world really is strange?"

Abby gave me an exasperated look. "That's only one of the diagnostic criteria. You have to meet a certain number of them to get a diagnosis."

I kept flipping. "According to this book, everyone must have some disorder or other. Seriously. This is even weirder than all those books on psychics."

She grabbed for the book. "This is *science*, Fiona. Psychologists and doctors use this book."

I flipped some more pages. *Depression, Anxiety, Obsessive-Compulsive Disorder. Complicated Grief Disorder.* I caught my breath and skimmed the next few lines. From the sounds of it, if someone died and you grieved too much or for too long, you got a diagnosis. What was too long? A year? A lifetime? And who got to decide? It reminded me of a brochure on grieving that a school counselor had given me, outlining the steps you were supposed to go through: denial, anger, bargaining and, finally, acceptance.

Only I didn't ever want to accept it. "This stuff is stupid," I said flatly. "Anyway, Kathy's not crazy. She's just a fake, that's all."

"So give it back then." Abby looked hurt.

I handed the book back. "Sorry," I muttered. "It's cool that you want to be a psychologist. And at least your mom is behind you."

"You're thinking about sailing, aren't you?" Abby gave me a sympathetic look. "Your dad's just worried about you."

"I know, but it's not like I'm planning to do anything dangerous. That's the whole point of learning: so that I can do it safely. If I'm going to sail to the South Pacific, I have to be prepared." I stood up, leaned against the school's brick wall and shoved my hands into my pockets.

"You'll need a boat." She looked at me. "If your dad sells *Eliza J*."

"I know," I said. I hadn't been to the marina all week. I was scared I might see an empty slip where our boat used to be.

Abby had that look on her face that meant she wanted to say something.

"What?" I asked.

"Nothing."

"Abby, come on. What is it?"

She sucked on her bottom lip for a second. "Don't get mad, okay?"

I sat back down on the step beside her. "Okay."

"Well, I was wondering…Your dad knows how much you want to sail, right?"

"Of course he does."

She hesitated. "He won't let you because of what happened to your mom, right?"

"Mostly, I guess. But he never really understood about sailing anyway." I thought about all the fights my parents had about it: about the expense, about safety, about *priorities.* That was the word that always came up, again and again, drifting into my bedroom on the updraft of their raised voices.

Peter, you know how much I've always wanted to do this. Doesn't that count for something? Don't you think all our dreams should be equally important?

I think your family should be your first priority, Dad had said.

Fiona doesn't mind. She understands how I feel about this.

Dad's voice was low and defeated. *We all understand how you feel, Jennifer. I just wish you would try to do some understanding yourself.*

"Maybe." Abby hesitated. "Maybe you should talk to him about it again. Try and explain how important it is to you."

The bell rang, and I stood up slowly. "I don't think so."

"Why not?"

I started walking up the steps to go back into the school. "I don't know, Abby. I don't think he'd want to talk about that."

Abby followed me. "It might be good for you both, you know."

"No. Drop it, Abby."

"It might be healing, you know? To talk about it."

I turned around, anger flashing up out of nowhere and exploding in my chest. "I said, drop it. Go play psychologist with someone else."

Abby's eyes widened, and her face flushed pink. She looked like I'd slapped her. "You know what, Fiona? Maybe I will. Maybe I'd rather hang out with someone who didn't bite my head off when I'm just trying to help."

My chest tightened and my breath caught. I didn't think I could stand to fight with Abby right now. "I'm sorry," I said awkwardly. "I didn't mean it."

She didn't look at me, and I could see that she was getting teary. "Sometimes I feel like I can't say anything right," she whispered. "You're so sensitive sometimes. I was only trying to help."

"I know. And if I wanted a psychologist, I'd pick you," I told her. "Honest."

"Okay." She gave me a tiny smile, but her eyes were still guarded.

My stomach hurt. I didn't understand why I kept pushing Abby away when I needed her so much. What if she got tired of putting up with me? "Come for dinner," I said. "I bet psycho woman will be there again."

She pulled out her phone to call her mom. "Then I'm there too."

fourteen

At dinner that night, I felt like a cat waiting to pounce on a mouse. I amused myself by asking Kathy questions about the future, dropping them into the conversation like little time bombs. So Kathy, you think it'll rain this weekend? Who do you think will win tonight's game? What do you think Dad's made for dessert? I was pretty sure she was no more likely to be right than anyone else. Still, even if she was 100 percent wrong, it wouldn't be enough to convince Dad.

Finally Kathy asked how school was going, and Abby made her move. She wiped her mouth with her napkin and leaned toward Kathy. "Fiona and I are doing this science project together," she said. "It's on psychic phenomena. I just think it's so interesting."

Kathy paused, her hand halfway to her mouth. She slowly lowered her slice of pizza back to her plate. "Do you?"

I watched her face carefully, trying to decipher her expression. Guarded, I decided. Wary.

"Oh yes," Abby assured her. "I've always thought so, but now that you and Fiona's dad are dating, that's practically like having a psychic in my own family."

That was going a bit too far. It wasn't like they were getting married or anything. I glanced over at Kathy and saw her reach for Dad's hand under the table.

"Anyway," Abby went on, "we've been doing this experiment to see if any of our friends have any psychic powers—telepathy or precognition—but so far, not a single person has."

Kathy nodded. "It's not common. I hope you weren't too disappointed."

I met Abby's eyes, gave her a tiny nod and held my breath. Do it, I thought. Ask her.

She bit her lip. "A little," she said sadly. "It would make our project a lot better." She gasped as if the idea had only just occurred to her. "Kathy? Would you take part in our experiment?"

There was a moment's silence, and Abby rushed to fill it. "It'll only take a few minutes. We just have to turn over the cards and you predict which ones will come up next. It's easy."

Watching Abby nod enthusiastically as she spoke, I felt a surge of hope. If only Kathy would agree, we'd be able to prove to Dad that she was no different than anyone else.

But Kathy shook her head. "I'm sorry to disappoint you girls," she said, "but those tests aren't sensitive enough to pick up most psychic phenomena. Besides, I never know what kind of messages the departed will bring me. Often it's only a few words or images. I don't always know what meaning they have, though the person I'm doing the reading for usually understands."

Waves. Bright lights. I'd understood, all right, and she knew it perfectly well. But at the same time, she had given herself a perfect excuse for failing the test. "That's a bit of a cop-out, don't you think?" I blurted.

Kathy's eyebrows flew up. "A *cop-out*?"

I could feel Dad's eyes burning holes in me, but I refused to look at him.

"Yeah. If you can't put your powers to a test, how do you know they're even real? How do you know you're not just imagining you have psychic powers?"

Kathy frowned. "I know it's probably hard for you to accept it. It's a new idea for you. It's unfamiliar—"

Anger flared inside me, and my words flew out, loud and sharp-edged. "Oh, so if I don't buy it, it means I'm just too narrow-minded, is that it?"

"Fiona!" Dad pushed his chair back from the table and stood up, eyebrows lowered warningly.

Kathy held out a hand toward him. "It's okay. She has a right to ask."

"Not like that, she doesn't."

"Peter, it's understandable that she's skeptical."

Dad grabbed my arm and yanked me to my feet. His fingers dug into my wrist. "Skeptical is fine," he said. "Disrespectful is not." He put his index finger under my chin and it so I had to look at him. "You owe Kathy an apology."

My eyes slid from his steady gaze and registered the circle of faces staring at me from around the table. Abby's round startled face, Caitlin's interested one—she was enjoying this, I thought—and finally Kathy's. She caught my eyes and gave me a tiny smile. If I hadn't known better, I'd have thought she looked almost sympathetic.

I hated lying, but Dad was still holding my arm and I had to say something. "Sorry if I said something I shouldn't have," I muttered. There. Not a lie. I didn't say anything I shouldn't have, and I wasn't sorry.

Dad let go of my arm, and I sat back down. Abby nudged my foot under the table, and I knew she wanted to cheer me up, but I just stared at my plate, cheeks burning. There was a long and very uncomfortable silence. The only sound was Caitlin chewing.

"It's okay, Fiona," Kathy said softly. "I understand. Honestly, I used to be skeptical about this sort of thing myself." She hesitated. "Listen, I don't know if you'd be interested at all, but I have an idea. I've got a booth at a psychic fair in Sidney tomorrow. Why don't you come? Both of you, I mean. See for yourselves what it's all about?"

Abby grabbed my arm. "Yes! We'd love to."

My heart sank at the thought of spending the next day with Kathy, but I couldn't say no: a chance to observe her at work was exactly what we'd been hoping for.

Kathy turned to Dad. "Is that okay? I'll be working, but Caitlin could introduce them to people; she knows everyone. It'd be a great opportunity for them to do some research for their project."

Dad shook his head. "You don't have to do that."

"I'd like to. Really." She sounded like she meant it.

He looked at me, his eyebrows pulled together and forehead knotted. "Do you want to go?"

I nodded, and he gave me a big relieved smile. I had to look away. If he knew the real reason I wanted to go, there was no way he'd agree.

It was a relief when the meal was finally over and Abby and I could escape to my bedroom.

"I *knew* she wouldn't let us test her," I said.

"Yeah. Tedium. Never mind though. It'll still be a great science project." She gestured toward our pile of notes and the poster board display we'd begun constructing. Green and purple letters on a black background spelled out *PSYCHIC PHENOMENA: FACT OR FICTION?*

"Whatever." As far as I was concerned, there was no point in the project if it didn't help me get Kathy out of my life.

Abby adjusted a slightly crooked border. "I bet we get an A on this."

I flopped onto my bed, ignoring the display. "Maybe the psychic fair will give us a chance to see what she does. See how she tricks people into believing she's communicating with dead people." I realized that I hadn't told Abby about Kathy's dead husband and daughter. Jack and Nicole. I opened my mouth to tell her.

"You know, Kathy seems nice," Abby said. "The psychic thing's weird, okay. But otherwise, don't you think she's all right?"

"Sure. But that's like saying she'd be okay if only she wasn't a big hypocrite and a fake. That's a pretty big *if only*."

"I guess," Abby said. She didn't sound convinced, and suddenly I was glad I hadn't told her about Jack and Nicole after all. I didn't want to give her a reason to feel sorry for Kathy.

I needed Abby on my side.

fifteen

The next day dawned bright and clear, with the kind of steady breeze that would fill sails without kicking up waves. I stood on the front porch and watched the soft white clouds floating high in the blue sky and the cherry blossoms fluttering from the trees and forming velvety pink drifts on the sidewalk. I could smell grass and damp earth and the clean salt tang of the ocean beneath it all.

A perfect sailing day.

If Mom was here, she'd have woken me up with a nudge and a grin. *Come on, get up. Life's too short to spend sunny days sleeping.* We'd take travel mugs of hot tea and get in the car, me grumbling about how early it was but not really minding, Mom quiet and smiling to herself, listening to CBC on the car radio as we headed down to the marina where *Eliza J* was waiting. I remembered how *Eliza J* would tug at her dock lines as the wind pushed her off the dock, and how Mom would laugh. *Look, she can't wait to be away.*

Kathy's car pulled up in front of my house, horn honking loudly. I shook my head, and the daydream shattered into pieces as sharp-edged and fragile as glass.

I got in the car and nodded hello. Kathy was wearing a straight black skirt, tall leather boots and a burgundy sweater. She said good morning, and Caitlin smiled at me, her pale hair damp and freshly combed. I smiled back automatically, but inside my head I was trying to catch hold of the fragments of memory. Mom's laugh, the smell of her perfume—*Paris.* She only ever wore that one kind, and I had her last half-empty bottle hidden in my T-shirt drawer. Sometimes I would put the tiniest drop on my pillow. I'd close my eyes and remember the way Mom used to nudge me with her elbow and look sideways at me, the way she said my name...

"Seven thirty sharp," Kathy said, giving me a crooked-toothed smile. "I didn't expect you to be ready. Thought I'd have to come and drag you out of bed."

"I like getting up early," I said.

"Well, it's sure nice weather," she said. "Pretty day for a drive."

The psychic fair was in Sidney, a half-hour drive. Mom and I used to sail there often. There was this long sandy bar—Sidney Spit—where we'd drop the anchor, eat some lunch and stroll on the beach. Sometimes, if a perfect sailing morning happened to dawn on a weekday, Mom would let me miss school to sail with her. *Days like this one don't come all the time. Carpe diem and all that good stuff. Besides, you'll learn more on a boat than they can ever teach you in a classroom.*

I wondered if I would always miss her like this—if the ache in my chest would be there forever. And then I realized that I didn't hurt like I did back in those first months after she disappeared, back when every breath felt like inhaling broken glass. I didn't think about her as much as I used to.

And somehow that made me feel worse instead of better.

*   *   *

We stopped to pick up Abby on the way. She flew out her front door, hair a tangle and shoes untied, half a peanut-buttered bagel in her hand.

"I overslept," she said, scrambling into the back seat beside me. She tried unsuccessfully to do up her seat belt with one hand; then she stuck the bagel in her mouth and held it between her teeth as she buckled herself in. "Okay! All set! Oh—I hope you don't mind me eating in the car."

Kathy shook her head, but you could tell by the way her lips tightened that she actually did mind. I grinned at Abby, and some of the knots inside me eased a little. Everything seemed more hopeful when your best friend was sitting beside you.

Already the smell of peanut butter was overpowering the shampoo and leather scent of Kathy's spotless car.

* * *

The psychic fair was in a big hall that reminded me of our school auditorium. I felt oddly disappointed: it was all so ordinary-looking. Tables and curtained-off areas were laid out in rows, forming four wide aisles lined with booths and shops.

Kathy glanced at her watch. "The doors don't officially open for another twenty minutes, but I have to get set up. Go ahead and wander around. Caitlin can introduce you to people."

We wandered down the first aisle, past tables spread with displays of books, jewelry, incense, crystals and a few things I didn't recognize. It was like a giant version of the Mystic Heart shop. Some people seemed to be selling stuff, but lots of the booths clearly featured psychics doing various kinds of readings. Brightly colored signs advertised their services: *Tarot cards! Palmistry! Numerology! Deep trance channeling!* These psychics sure liked their exclamation points.

"Check this out," Abby whispered, handing me a flyer. "Past-life readings."

Large blocky letters tripped across pastel paper. "'Past-life readings,'" I read aloud. "'Only by understanding and healing our past-life experiences can we move freely forward into a joyful future.'"

Abby started to laugh, snorting slightly.

"'Free emotional energy and resolve karmic debt,'" I continued. "'Only by discovering our past selves can we truly, at a cellular level, liberate our innermost souls and embrace the present.'" I shook my head. "Whoa. This makes Kathy look halfway normal."

Abruptly, Abby stopped laughing. She grabbed my arm. "Shhh, Fi!"

I'd forgotten that Caitlin was standing about two feet away. She was looking at Abby and me, and I couldn't read the expression on her face at all. "Sorry," I told her quickly. Dad would kill me if Caitlin repeated what I'd said.

Caitlin dropped her eyes, adjusting her pink plastic belt and tucking the end into an embroidered belt loop. After a few uncomfortable seconds, she glanced up at me, her eyes a flicker of blue behind long pale lashes. "You don't believe in this stuff, do you? Mediums, psychics...any of this."

I shook my head. "Nope. Not really."

"Mom doesn't do past-life readings," she said. "She says understanding our present lives is plenty hard enough."

Abby stuck the past-lives flyer in her jeans pocket. "So what exactly does your mom do?" she asked innocently.

"She's a medium. She can connect with people who have gone beyond. And she's a clairvoyant too. She knows things about people. It's like...you know how we all have intuition about things?"

Abby nodded. "Sure."

"Well, Mom's intuition is amazing. She picks up on how people are feeling, and she can tell all kinds of stuff about their lives."

Abby looked thoughtful. "She'd probably make a good psychologist."

I snorted. "Yeah. Right."

Caitlin looked at me, her chin lifted and her eyes full of challenge. For some reason, I remembered her saying my dad was too old for her mom, and for a second I wondered what it was like for her having a mom like Kathy. Not to mention a dead father and sister who passed on messages for her.

"You should get a reading," Caitlin said. "See for yourselves."

"As if I'd waste my money." I guessed that meant Kathy hadn't told Caitlin about our earlier meeting.

"Actually, it's not a bad idea." Abby gave me a meaningful look. "In the interest of science, Fi. Research."

Caitlin looked pleased. "You want me to introduce you to some people? Mom's friend Ruth reads auras. Or Deirdre. You could get her to do a reading for you. She's a clairvoyant like my mom."

Abby shook her head decisively. "I want your mom to do it for me. You think she would? I brought money."

"I'll go ask." Caitlin rushed off, her cheeks as pink as her Hello Kitty T-shirt.

"Abby." I scrunched my nose up like something smelled bad. "Are you serious?"

"Sure. We weren't on the alert before, but this time we'll be prepared. We have to watch for tricks. Scams. Like, this one psychic I read about had a bunch of people secretly working for her, like spies. So when a particular customer came up for a reading, this psychic might already know her name,

what kind of day she was having, even what she was
hoping to find out."

I looked around at the people milling around in
the aisles and wondered which of them might be spies.
Kathy's spies. "Kathy already knows a fair bit about
you," I pointed out. "She's got an advantage, doing a
reading for someone she knows."

"Someone she thinks she knows," Abby said.

We headed in the direction of Kathy's booth. She
and Caitlin were talking, so we stopped and browsed
at a booth a short distance away. A black-velvet-
covered table was laid out with a carefully arranged
display of crystals and a few copies of a book
entitled *Crystals: Power, Healing, Enlightenment*.
I picked one up and turned it over to read the back.
A large color photo was displayed prominently:
a beaming, balding man with a large fleshy nose and
protruding teeth.

"Guess crystals fix everything but overbites," Abby
whispered in my ear.

I snorted, looked up and saw that same beaming
face gazing right at me, over Abby's shoulder.

"Hush," I said quickly. "Don't look now, but it's his
booth. The author."

Abby almost spun to look, but managed to resist
the urge. "Oops," she said. "He didn't hear me?"

"Not a chance." Out of the corner of my eye, I could see Kathy shaking her head. "I think she's going to refuse," I whispered to Abby. "Maybe she knows you don't believe in it either."

A large hand descended onto the table in front of me, and I looked up, startled. It was the balding buck-toothed man who wrote the crystals book, and he was smiling widely at us.

"Can I answer any questions for you?" he asked. "Or perhaps you'd like to look at my DVDs? All the information that's in the book, in an easy-to-understand two-hour presentation."

I leaned to one side, trying to see past him to Kathy. He was blocking my view. "Just browsing," I said.

Abby was trying to edge away, but Crystal Man had already spotted her.

"Now this crystal here, that you were looking at, is called citrine. Very good for acid indigestion, food disorders, allergies. Also it helps to cleanse the spleen, kidneys, liver, urinary system and intestines."

Abby shook her head. "No, thanks. I'm fine, really."

"Yeah, her internal organs are very clean already," I added, grabbing her arm. "Come on, Abby, we should go."

"You should look at this one here," Crystal Man said enthusiastically. "Hold it, go on." He thrust a purple stone into my hand.

I tried to hand it back. "Really, we have to go."

"Amethyst," he said, not taking it from me. "Very powerful stone, good balancing energy. Helps keep your blood sugar steady. Also very good for your eyes, preventing headaches." He lowered his voice. "And it reduces irritability too."

Abby stifled a giggle, and I glared at her. I didn't need any psychic powers to know what she was thinking. I grabbed her arm. "Excuse us," I said. "We're here with Kathy." I nodded toward her booth as I backed away. "Thanks for all the information."

Giggling, Abby followed me toward Kathy's table. "Loopy!" she said. "Completely loopy."

"No loopier than talking to dead people," I reminded her.

Kathy and Caitlin had stopped talking and were sitting in wooden chairs behind the table. Kathy had hung a banner that read simply *Kathy Morrison: Medium and Clairvoyant Empath*. No exclamation marks, no black velvet. She looked tired: gray circles under her eyes and deep lines around her mouth. The straggly locks of dark hair escaping from her ponytail didn't help.

She smiled when she saw us. "Caitlin says you want a reading."

Abby nodded and pulled out her wallet. "I'd love one. I've never done this before."

"In that case, I'd be honored. No charge."

There was a sudden increase in the noise level, and I looked behind me. The doors had just opened, and people were starting to stream in.

"You want to go first and beat the lineups?" Kathy asked. "Or are you going to wander around some more and think it over?"

Abby grinned. "I'll go first," she said. "I can hardly wait."

sixteen

Abby sat down across the small table from Kathy. I watched, wondering if Kathy was going to chant or pull out a crystal ball or do anything weird and embarrassing. She didn't though—she just sat there quietly for a moment, like she'd done with me at the Mystic Heart. She watched Abby with that expression people get when they watch television: interested, but also sort of zoned out.

After a minute or two, she sighed. "Abby, would you mind if I held your hand? Sometimes physical contact helps me pick up more from a person."

Abby stuck her hand out, and Kathy took it and held it lightly in her own. I was glad I hadn't volunteered. The thought of holding hands with Kathy made me queasy.

"Hmmm…You are an open-minded person," Kathy said slowly. "Willing to try out new ideas, ready for new experiences."

I tried not to snort. Duh. Obviously, since she was here getting a psychic reading. I wondered if it was meant as a dig at me for being closed-minded.

"You have a strong sense of who you are and what you want. You make your own decisions and are not easily influenced by others. You see the best in people…" Kathy cleared her throat. "You have high expectations and sometimes feel let down by the people you care about."

Me? Was she talking about me and my lousy grades? I had to remind myself that it was all made up: vague general statements that could mean anything. Exactly like it said in the books we had read.

"I get a strong sense that you are very intuitive… very insightful."

Ha. That was another classic technique that we'd read about: compliment the client. I tried to catch Abby's eye, but she was grinning at Kathy. "I want to be a psychologist," she told her.

"Ah. Yes, you would do that well." Kathy looked at Abby's hand for a long minute. "I also sense a deep spiritual side to you. A strong potential. I wonder. Do you have some psychic abilities yourself?"

Abby shook her head, wide-eyed. For some reason, I picked that moment to glance over at Caitlin. Her arms were folded across her chest, her mouth pulled tight in a scowl, and I remembered what Kathy had said the day we went shopping. *Caitlin is a bit sad about not having my abilities.* No wonder Caitlin didn't like hearing her mom say that Abby—who didn't even believe this stuff—might have potential.

Kathy released Abby's hand. She closed her eyes and touched her fingertips to her temples. Her voice changed, becoming lower and almost sleepy. I wondered if she was going into a trance or something. "I'm getting a message from someone," she said slowly. "Is there someone you know who has passed on?"

Abby shrugged. "My grandmother, I guess. And"— she looked over at me apologetically—"well, Fiona's mom."

My heart started to beat fast. Ask her. Ask her if she can speak to my mom. Ask if my mom has a message for me.

Kathy's eyes were still closed, her face relaxed. "An older woman, small. Gray-haired."

"Gran!" Abby sat straight up. "That's Gran."

I stared at her, willing her to look my way, wanting to remind her that Kathy was a fake. It didn't take a psychic to guess that her grandmother might have had gray hair. But Abby's gaze was locked on Kathy's face.

"She isn't saying anything, but I sense a strong love for you, a concern."

"We were really close," Abby said. "She died two years ago."

"She's present, but on a higher plane. She's thinking of you. She's saying something, but I can't quite hear her. Something about a beach? Does that make any sense?"

"We used to go to the beach together," Abby said. "She collected stones. She had a stone tumbler and she made jewelry."

"She loves you very much."

"Yes. She did."

"Oh, she still does." Kathy opened her eyes. "That's all, I think. She wants you to know that she loves you."

Abby didn't say anything. She was looking a bit stunned. "That was amazing. Gran…jeez."

I wanted to shake her. Surely she didn't believe Kathy just because of a couple of lucky guesses? I couldn't stand it. I had to do something. "My turn," I said.

Kathy and Abby both turned and looked at me.

"Seriously?" Abby asked.

My chest felt tight, but I moved closer. "Sure, why not?"

Abby stood and moved to one side. I took the seat and met Kathy's eyes. "So?"

Kathy hesitated. "I can try. But it doesn't always work if you aren't open to it."

Cop-out. "I'm open to it," I said flatly. I didn't know if it was true or not. I didn't believe her. But I wanted to. More than anything, I wanted to.

Kathy leaned toward me. I could feel her eyes examining my face, and I had to force myself to sit still. *Mom,* I called silently. *If you are out there…please please please please please…*

"I sense a deep hurt…a loss." Kathy's voice was soft.

I snorted. "Well, duh."

"Sorry, I know that must sound like I'm stating the obvious, but it's what comes across most overwhelmingly." She closed her eyes for a moment. "Anger. I can't always see auras, but I can see yours. There's a place you think of sometimes that brings you a sense of calm, of peace. Does that make sense?"

The marina. Eliza J.

"Yes," Kathy said. "You just thought of it and your aura shifted from reds to blues and greens."

A shiver prickled across the base of my spine. I folded my arms across my chest. "What else?"

She held out her hands for mine, and I turned one palm up toward her reluctantly. I shivered, remembering the palm reader talking to my mother at the fair. *You will still be traveling when you are an old woman.*

Kathy took my hand between hers and gazed at it. Her hands were cool and smooth, slender-fingered, her nails expertly French-manicured. Mom's were always rough with calluses, her nails cut short. Practical hands. Hands that raised sails and tied knots and baked cookies and fixed engines.

She leaned closer. "Who is Michael?"

I shrugged. "Dunno." I didn't think I knew any Michaels.

"Well, I'm seeing the name very clearly. He could be from your past or your future. Is there a Michael at school perhaps? I sense that he has some significance in your life. Maybe someone who wants to get to know you? An admirer?"

I snorted and shook my head. *Nice try, Kathy.* It was so transparent. So fake. The line about how something could be from your past or your future. Well, that pretty much covered her for every wrong guess.

Kathy smiled. "I see something else. I see you and Abby in a room full of people. A school gym, perhaps. An older woman talking to you and smiling."

Mrs. Moskin? She didn't usually smile at me.

"She's congratulating you...Does this sound familiar? It could be past or future."

Behind me, I heard Abby gasp. "I bet we've aced our science project!"

"Yes, maybe. I see a red letter A…"

I interrupted her. "What about my mom? Can you see her? Does she have a message for me?"

"Oh. Oh, dear." Kathy sat back, frowning. "Fiona, I can't try to contact your mother."

"Why not? You contacted Abby's grandmother."

"Yes, but…"

"I'm open to it! I am!" Tears were stinging my eyes, and I could taste their salt, but I would not cry in front of Kathy. I would *not*.

"I know you are. It's not that."

"So why not? Can't you ask someone? Ask Nicole. Can't she give you a message?"

Kathy touched my shoulder lightly. "Fiona. I promised your father I wouldn't."

I stared at her. "My father?"

She nodded.

"Have you given him messages from my mom? What did she say? Do you know what happened to her? Does Dad believe in all this? He never used to believe this sort of stuff." My words were tumbling out, my thoughts a tornado of memories and questions.

Kathy shook her head. "You'll have to ask him yourself."

"Tell me. Please." If Dad didn't believe her, why was he with her? And if he did…if he did believe her, surely he'd want to contact Mom. And if he was in contact with my mother—if he was actually getting *messages* from her—why wouldn't he share that with me? I'd give anything for even one word from her. One single word.

"Fiona, I'm sorry. It's not my place to go against his wishes. You talk to him later, okay?" Kathy looked past me at the lineup forming on the other side of her table. Paying customers. "I better get to work. You two go have some fun."

I stood there staring at her as she walked over and shook hands with a young woman with a green and orange scarf tied over black hair. Finally Abby grabbed my arm. "Fi. Come on."

I shook off the arm and followed her away from Kathy's table and down the first aisle, back past Crystal Man and the past-life booth.

"Wow," Abby said. "That wasn't what I expected."

"No? Seemed about right to me," I said. "Leading questions, general statements that could be interpreted in any number of ways."

"But that stuff about my gran…"

"You told her yourself that your gran was dead. All she did was guess that she had gray hair and that she loved you." I raised my eyebrows. "That's a pretty safe guess."

"The part about the beach though. We used to go to the beach together."

"Yeah, along with half the people in Victoria. We're surrounded by beaches. Besides, it could have meant that she lived near a beach or grew up near one, or that you had a picnic on a beach once. It could have been anything."

"I guess." Abby didn't sound convinced.

"And if it meant nothing to you, she'd have thrown out something else. A flower, maybe, or a Christmas tree, or a teacup. Sooner or later, she's going to hit on something. You were the one making the connections, not her."

"You're upset because she wouldn't try to contact your mom, aren't you?"

I stuck my hands in my pockets. "I don't get it. Why would Dad tell her not to? Do you think he really believes this stuff?"

"He must. He'd hardly be dating her if he thought she was a liar, right?"

I snorted. "She is a liar. She's either lying to him or— if she really believes this stuff—she's lying to herself."

Abby shook her head. "I don't know, Fi. I thought so too, but she's pretty convincing."

"Yeah, right. And I suppose that if I ever meet anyone called Michael—which, by the way, is a pretty common name—it's going to be more evidence that Kathy is for real. That was a classic technique, Abby. It's right out of one of those library books."

"What about the science-project thing?" Abby said defensively. "How'd she know about that?"

"You're the one who said it was our science project. You *gave* her the answers, Abby. All she said was that some woman was smiling at us in a gym. It could have been anything."

"A red letter A. You know Mrs. Moskin always uses red ink."

I stamped my foot. "Abby! That was after you told her it might be our science project. And most teachers use red ink." An idea was slowly forming in my mind. "Besides, I can make sure we don't get an A. I won't hand my stuff in on time. Or I'll make a ton of little mistakes. I won't bother underlining headings, and I'll spell things wrong and…"

Abby grabbed my shoulder and spun me around to face her. "Don't you dare, Fiona! That's my grade too, remember?"

I shrugged. "If you're so sure that Kathy's psychic, what are you worried about? She said you'll get an A."

"I can't believe you'd even consider messing up our science project because Kathy suggested we'd get an A." Abby screwed her mouth down to one side and shook her head. "That's so wrong."

"I won't do it, okay? I'm just saying I could."

"Yeah. You could wreck your own grades—and your best friend's. Nice, Fi. Real nice."

"You're missing my point," I said, raising my voice. "Which is, Kathy doesn't know everything, okay? She can't control what I do, so her predictions don't mean anything."

Caitlin's soft voice cut in. "Mom says it's a chancy business. She says the future isn't written in stone. That we all have free will and can alter the course of events by our actions."

So proving Kathy wrong wouldn't help me either. She had an answer—an excuse—for everything. "How long have you been standing there listening?" I asked, scowling at her. "We were having a private conversation."

"Could have fooled me," Caitlin said. "You were practically shouting at Abby."

"I was not."

Abby looked at me. "Yeah, actually you were, Fiona."

"Go ahead, take Caitlin's side. You've already taken Kathy's side anyway."

"I have not!"

"You only liked her because she said you were intuitive. You think that wasn't deliberate?" I knew my words would hurt her, but I didn't care. "She tells you you'd be a good psychologist, and you're so desperate to believe her that you forget every single thing we've read about how this works. Some researcher you are."

Abby was staring at me like I was a stranger, and I couldn't meet her eyes. My heart was thumping, and I could feel sweat trickling down my back. I looked around the room at all the people lining up and whispering and hoping and pretending to hope, and I hated myself for being a part of it. I wished Joni was here. She wouldn't be tricked by a few lucky guesses and a flattering description of her personality.

I wanted to scream. Or cry. Or throw something. If I didn't get out of here, I was going to lose it in front if everyone. I was going to grab Crystal Man's stupid rocks and hurl them at Abby and Kathy and all the other idiots and phonies in this stupid place. "I'm going out for a few minutes," I said. "You guys go ahead and get your auras read or whatever."

I could hear Abby protesting as I walked away, but I didn't look back.

seventeen

I stepped outside, and the sun shone straight in my eyes, dizzyingly bright. Away from the hum and stuffiness of the crowded hall, the air was cool and fresh. I walked quickly down Beacon Avenue, lifted my face to the breeze and smelled the musky salt smell of the ocean. Sidney-by-the-Sea is what the tourist brochures called this town. When Mom and I sailed to Sidney Spit, we usually went to the beach, explored the rocky, wind-swept cliffs and had lunch in *Eliza J*'s cockpit, but sometimes we took the little ferry to Sidney and wandered around the marine shops and bookstores. We ate halibut tacos and chips at Fish on Fifth and browsed the thrift stores for secondhand board games. Everywhere I looked, I was reminded of Mom, and I realized that this was the first time I'd been here since she died.

I made my way down to the waterfront and sat down on the grass, hugging my knees to my chest. There were lots of boats out today: small sailboats, their sails making sharp white triangles against the dark water; the harbor ferry chugging along; a couple of powerboats zipping toward Victoria. I closed my eyes and pictured *Eliza J* in the spot we always anchored, just off the spit. She was a heavy boat, with a full keel, and she sat at anchor more solidly than a lot of other boats. Mom and I would watch the lighter fin-keeled boats moving from side to side with the wind, and Mom would say, *She may not be fast, but* Eliza J *is the kind of boat you want in a storm. She's a boat you could cross the ocean in.* And she'd wink at me, knowing I was planning to do exactly that.

What if the new people, the people who bought her, took her away somewhere? It would be awful enough to see other people sailing her out of our marina all summer, but what if the new people lived in Vancouver or Port Hardy or on the Sunshine Coast? I'd never see *Eliza J* again.

I had to see her. Even if the worst happened and she was sold and taken away somewhere, I had to see her at least once more. I had to say goodbye.

I stood up, brushed the damp grass from my jeans and walked along the seawall, watching the boats and the water, hoping to see a seal poking its head out of the waves. Even this early in the season, there were lots of people around. Tourists with cameras dangling around their necks and maps clutched in their hands, half of them eating ice creams or greasy fries from paper cones. I wished I had some money. I was starving.

I knew I should go back to the hall, but I couldn't stand the thought of returning to that big airless room. It was totally creepy: all those people pretending that the dead weren't gone forever, pretending that they hung around, invisible but close by, waiting to send messages back just as long as their loved ones shed some cash along with their tears. The whole psychic scene made me sick, and I couldn't believe Abby had been sucked right into it.

So I didn't go back. I just walked around, looking at boats, watching the waves and trying not to think about anything at all.

"Fiona!" A voice cut through my thoughts, and I spun around. Kathy, flanked by Abby and Caitlin. "What were you *thinking*?" The wind blew Kathy's hair across her face. She tucked it behind her ears roughly. "You've been gone for hours. I was beside myself."

I shrugged. "Should've used your psychic powers to find me."

Her mouth tightened into a pale ugly line, and she looked as if she wanted to slap me. I almost wished she would lose her cool and do it. Then at least I would have something to tell Dad.

"Abby guessed where you'd be." She shook her head, and her hair escaped from behind her ears and whipped across her face again. "Your dad trusted me to look after you, and the second I turn my back, you run away."

"I didn't run away," I protested. "I went for a walk. To get some fresh air. I'd have come back. It's not like Sidney is New York or anything."

"I'm taking you home." She started walking, striding off in front of me, her boot heels clicking against the sidewalk cement. "Come on."

Abby caught my eye. "Sorry," she whispered. "She asked me where you were, and I didn't know what to say."

"I suppose you're a believer now," I said. "I suppose you're on her side."

Abby's face got that wobbly look that comes right before someone starts crying. "I don't know what to believe," she said.

Traitor. I kept walking, following Kathy to the car.

We got into the car and headed onto the highway back to Victoria. No one spoke. I could see Kathy's fingers drumming furiously against the wheel. I'd bet her aura was an ugly color right about now.

When we were halfway home, Kathy stopped at a red light and twisted in her seat to face me. "Did you run off because I wouldn't try to contact your mother? Because I can see how that might upset you, but I can't go against your father's wishes. Surely you can understand that?"

"It's not like I believe in this stuff anyway," I said sullenly.

She sighed. "Being in contact with Nicole brought me such comfort. I'd love to give that to you, Fiona. I really would. But you have to talk to your father about it first. Would you do that?"

I couldn't imagine that conversation. *So, Dad, is it okay if your psychic girlfriend passes on the odd message from Mom? Any objections to me getting back in touch with her?* "Do you give him messages from my mother?" I asked her.

She turned to face forward as the light turned green. "Talk to him, Fiona. Talk to him."

Abby cleared her throat. "Who's Nicole?"

Uh-oh. I bit my lip and looked out the window. I should've known that story would come out eventually.

"My daughter. My older daughter." Kathy sounded surprised. "She died in a car accident with my husband. Nicole's my guide in the spirit world. Didn't Fiona tell you?"

"No," Abby said. Her voice was very quiet. "No, she didn't tell me."

I turned to look at Abby. She was staring at me thoughtfully, and I could tell that she knew exactly why I hadn't told her. "Sorry," I mouthed.

She shook her head and looked away. Neither of us spoke the rest of the way home, and when we dropped Abby off at her house, she didn't even say goodbye.

eighteen

I headed straight to my room. I figured Dad would give me a lecture as soon as Kathy had a chance to fill him in. I couldn't decide whether I should ask him about letting Kathy try to contact Mom. Since I didn't believe she could do it, it seemed stupid to ask. Still, there was that nagging possibility that I couldn't leave alone. *What if she could?* I kept poking at that question the way you poke at a bruise, checking to see if it still hurts.

Sure enough, not more than five minutes had gone by before I heard Dad's footsteps pounding up the stairs. He opened my door without knocking first.

"So." He sat down beside me on the edge of my bed. "I guess you don't need me to tell you that Kathy was pretty upset by what you did."

"I didn't do anything. I went for a walk, that's all. I needed fresh air." I stood up and moved away from him, walking a few steps to lean against my dresser. "She made this huge deal out of it." A car door slammed and an engine started. I hoped that was the sound of Kathy leaving.

Dad took off his glasses and started wiping the lenses with the bottom of his shirt. "She said you asked her to contact your mom."

"She was doing readings for us. She said she had a message from Abby's gran."

He kept polishing his glasses, working at it as if he was trying to wear a hole right through the lens. "I asked her not to get into that kind of thing with you. Thought it wouldn't be helpful."

"Thought *what* wouldn't be helpful, Dad? Being lied to? Or talking to Mom?" I raised my voice. "Do you believe Kathy? Has she given you messages?"

Dad didn't say anything for a long time. His eyes were pink and watery, and his mouth got this odd wavy look, sort of uncertain and shaky. "Fiona…"

I waited.

"I worry that it isn't helpful for you. Thinking about this kind of thing. Better for you to try to move on with your life."

"Tell me the truth," I said. "Please. I need to know."

He put his glasses back on, glanced up at me, took them off again. "I don't know what I believe," he said at last. "I've always been a practical sort of person, but Kathy does seem to know things sometimes. And the world is full of mysteries that defy explanation. You know that."

I didn't want to get off on a tangent about Stonehenge or crop circles. "Has she given you messages?" I asked again. "Has she said she can talk to Mom?"

"Look, I don't want you talking to other people about this, okay? Or making too much of it." He cleared his throat. "She gave me a message the first time I met her. She said that your mom wanted me to know that she was okay. She was happy. And she said that it was okay for me to move on."

"Jesus, Dad—"

"Don't swear."

"—that is such bull. Mom wouldn't be happy without us. You know she wouldn't." My chest got tight. "And telling you that it was okay to move on? Duh. Of course she'd say that if she wanted to, you know, go out with you."

I expected him to be angry, but he just looked sort of sad and defeated. "I don't know what to say, Fiona. I haven't asked Kathy to get in touch with Jennifer again. In fact, we haven't talked much about her…her communications. Not since that one time. Because…" He cleared his throat again. "Because I don't know what to think about all this. But I do know that Kathy is a kind and intelligent woman who genuinely wants to help people. Who *does* help people."

"She's a liar. A big fake." I thought about what Kathy had said the first time I met her—about the waves and the bright lights and the fear—but I didn't want to tell Dad anything that might lend support to her claims.

He shook his head. "She believes in what she does. That much I know for sure. Her daughter, Nicole…"

"She told me."

"Oh, honey." Dad's forehead creased, and his face got this crumpled sort of look. "To lose your partner *and* your child. I don't think I'd have survived that. Having you to take care of was the only thing that kept me going."

I swallowed, and it felt like a knife was lodged in my throat. I thought about all those weeks last spring when I stayed with Joni because Dad was so depressed and how sometimes I'd felt like Dad hadn't even noticed that I was still around. "How did you meet her?" I asked at last.

His neck flushed red and blotchy. "I picked up her business card somewhere. Made an appointment."

I stared at him. "Seriously? I mean, because she was, because she said she was a medium?"

He nodded. "You know, your mom wasn't as much of a skeptic as you and me."

"Mom didn't believe this stuff." I remembered the palm reader at the fair. "She thought it was fun. A laugh. Not something serious."

"She used to have this Ouija board. When we were first married, she and her girlfriends would pull it out every weekend, more or less. They'd drink wine, get all giggly. Ask it questions, I guess."

"Like what? What kind of questions?"

"Oh, I don't know. Girl stuff, she said. They always kicked me out." Dad laughed softly. "I don't think Jennifer took it seriously. Still, when I saw Kathy's card, I just thought, why not? Why not try it?"

I wanted him to keep talking about Mom. Not Kathy. "Because you missed her so much."

"And because things were very unresolved between us. We fought before she left on that trip. Well, you know that. Your mother and I…we both said things we shouldn't have said."

I wondered what would have happened if Mom hadn't died. Would she have come back to us? Or were she and Dad heading toward divorce? But I didn't really want to know the answer.

"When your mom didn't come back, I kept thinking about that last fight. I never said goodbye properly to her, didn't tell her I loved her before she left." He looked at me. "I really did love her, you know."

I swallowed hard. "I know you did."

"I guess when I saw Kathy's card, it seemed like a chance to say goodbye, somehow." He sighed. "Whether the message came from your mom or not, it's the truth. I do have to move on."

Forget about Mom. It seemed to me that was what people meant when they said *move on.* "Dad? About *Eliza J...*"

"There's no point in holding on to your mom's boat any longer." He shook his head. "You have to move on too, Fiona. She's not coming back."

*   *   *

I ate mac n' cheese alone at the kitchen table. Dad went out with Kathy to have dinner at some fancy new Moroccan place. I hated thinking about the two of them together, talking, laughing, eating. Doing their best to erase every last trace of my mother.

It would be so much easier to deal with someone dying if you believed they weren't gone forever, that they were just elsewhere. On a higher plane, as Kathy said. *In a better place.* That was what Abby's Mom always said about Abby's gran. *We miss her, but she's in a better place now.* Sometimes I envied people who believed in things.

I kept looking at the phone and wishing Abby would call, but I couldn't blame her if she didn't. Finally I picked up the phone and dialed her number.

"Abby? It's me."

"Oh. Hi." Her voice was stiff.

"Look, I was wondering about your gran. About how you think she's in heaven?"

"You know what, Fiona? I don't really feel like talking about it."

"Oh. Sorry, I didn't mean to…"

"I have to go," Abby said.

I tightened my grip on the phone. "Abby, wait a minute. What's wrong?"

"Seriously, Fiona? You don't know?"

"I'm sorry I didn't tell you about Kathy's daughter, if that's what you mean."

"It's not just that, Fi."

"What is it then?" My chest was suddenly tight.

"Look, I know your mom died and I'm sorry, okay? But I'm tired of you being so mean all the time."

"Abby. I'm sorry, okay?"

She was quiet for a moment. "You always say you're sorry, Fiona."

"But I am sorry! I really am!" I started to cry and quickly slid my hand over the phone so she wouldn't hear me.

"My mom says I should be patient, but you know what? I'm kind of tired of being patient. It's been a year, Fiona."

I was crying too hard to speak, and besides, what more was there to say? I listened to the silence coming over the phone for a few seconds; then I hung up, ran into my room and threw myself on my bed. Everything good in my life seemed to be slipping away: Mom, *Eliza J* and now Abby too.

I rolled over and looked at the photographs on my bulletin board. Me and Abby sitting on the grass, me and Abby wearing Santa hats, me and Abby with our arms around each other. I wiped the tears from my eyes. Kathy had stolen Abby as well as Dad, and I didn't think I could stand it.

Though in some ways, I felt like I'd lost Dad even before Kathy came along. He was so distant, and sometimes I wondered if he blamed me for what happened to my mother. If I'd begged her to take more safety precautions, she might have listened. But I didn't even try. I just took her side like I always did. Dad never invited me to take sides, but Mom... I felt sort of disloyal for thinking it, but the truth was that if I didn't take her side, my mother got all quiet and sulky and hurt. She needed me on her side more than Dad did.

But Dad had been right. She should have taken precautions. Or not gone at all.

Tonight had been the first time in ages that Dad had talked about my mom. The Ouija board stuff was before I was born, but I could imagine it, could picture her laughing about it the way she had about the palm reader we'd seen together. Not really believing it, but having fun all the same.

I rolled over on the bed. If Mom wanted to get in touch with me, and if such a thing was possible, then I didn't need Kathy. *Mom* didn't need Kathy. Why would Mom choose to talk to a woman who was dating her husband when she could talk to me directly?

It took me all of five minutes to find the Ouija board. It was in the crawl space in a box labeled *Games*, along with an old Monopoly set and a bunch of jigsaw puzzles. I pulled it out and took it up to my bedroom.

A beige plastic board, with the letters of the alphabet on it. Also the words *yes, no* and *maybe*. It looked oddly familiar, and I wondered if I might have played with it before, when I was little. I pulled a little triangular pointer out of the box and placed it on the board with a soft *click*. Then I turned off the overhead light in my room and lit a candle, even though it felt like kind of a dumb thing to do. If my mother was able to contact me from some spirit world, I didn't really think that the lighting in the room was going to make much difference.

I sat cross-legged on my bed and rested my fingers lightly on the smooth plastic of the pointer. Mom, I thought. Mom…if you are out there…if you can talk to me…

Nothing happened. I thought maybe I should ask a question, but I didn't know where to begin. I had so many. Why did you leave us? What happened? Was it really a navigational error? Are you still out there somewhere? On a tropical island? In a spirit world with Kathy's dead husband and daughter and Abby's gran? How am I supposed to get by without you? Do you think it's okay that I still want to sail?

In the end I just stayed quiet. It slowly grew darker outside, and after a very long time my legs started to cramp. Nothing had happened. No movement beneath my fingers, no whispered words, no chill breeze disturbing the air. Not the slightest sign. I pushed the pointer, sliding it over to the letter *I*. Then *M. I. S. S. Y. O. U. I miss you.*

I stood up stiffly, walked over to the window, slid it open and pushed my nose against the screen. Dad's car wasn't back yet. "I love you, Mom," I whispered. My voice disappeared into the night air. I stood there for a long moment, and an awful aching certainty settled deep inside me. If Mom could have answered me, she would have done so. I knew that was true.

Kathy was wrong. Mom wasn't waiting on the other side of some invisible curtain. She wasn't hanging out on some social networking site for dead people, or watching over me like a guardian angel. She was dead. She was gone.

She's not coming back, Dad had said. And I knew that was true too.

nineteen

I woke before the sun came up. The square of sky outside my window was still dark, and beside my bed my alarm clock flashed 5:29. I pulled on jeans, a sweatshirt and a fleece jacket, and tiptoed downstairs.

Dad always slept in on Sunday mornings, usually until eight thirty or nine, so I had at least three hours to myself.

I needed to see *Eliza J.*

I grabbed an apple from the fridge, headed outside and stopped dead. Kathy's car was in the driveway, parked right behind ours. She'd stayed the night.

I didn't want to think about that or what it meant.

My bike was in the backyard, locked to the fence. I unlocked it silently and wheeled it past the cars and out to the street. I wondered if Caitlin had a babysitter, or if she was at home alone. I wondered what she thought of Kathy spending the night with my father. I bet she hated it about as much as I did.

Just above the horizon, wide streaks as creamy white as sails were starting to light up the darkness. I swung my leg over the seat of my bike and pedaled off down the street toward the marina.

The sun was a tangerine semicircle emerging from a low bank of cloud, and the wind blew steadily through the deserted marina. I locked my bike to the rack and walked down the ramp to the water. Low tide. I listened to the clang and clatter of the wind blowing loose halyards against aluminum masts, the call of a gull swooping low overhead, the groan of dock lines pulling taut against their steel cleats.

As I turned onto E-dock, I could see the faded blue of *Eliza J*'s sail cover. I hurried toward her and stepped on board. A halyard shackle clanked against the mast with a gentle chime, as if *Eliza J* was welcoming me back.

"Are you happy to see me?" I said softly. "Beautiful boat. I've missed you." Mom was gone, Dad was with Kathy, Abby didn't want to be my friend anymore, but *Eliza J* had always been there for me. And I hadn't visited her for so long. Poor *Eliza J*. I ran my hand along the edge of the dodger, feeling the roughness of the tightly stretched canvas—and stopped abruptly as something caught my eye. The For Sale sign at her bow had been flipped over, a line drawn through the price. I leaned over the railing to get a look at the side of the sign visible from the dock.

SOLD.

I sank down to the cockpit bench and pushed my hands against my ears, trying to muffle the roaring noise, even though I knew it was coming from inside my head. *Sold.* Dad must have known it last night and been too much of a coward to tell me. Or too busy maybe, too distracted, off for dinner with his stupid, lying hypocrite of a girlfriend. Who was, presumably, lying in his bed right now.

My nails dug into my palms, and my stomach clenched as tight as my fists. I wished I could go down below into the cabin and curl up on my old berth. I looked at the companionway boards and the padlock that held them firmly in place. It seemed so wrong that I was locked out. I turned away, blinking back tears, and looked out at the water. I wished I could sail away. I imagined standing at the helm, feeling the power of the wind lifting the sails, listening to the sound of the hull moving through the water, seeing the sea stretching out before me forever.

Standing up, I slid the blue canvas tube off the tiller, wanting to feel the smooth wood under my hand one more time. The canvas cover slipped from my hand and dropped onto the locker lid, making an oddly heavy clunking sound. I picked it up and ran my fingers along the inch-wide seam at the bottom edge.

There it was: the spare key Mom had kept hidden inside the seam of the tiller cover ever since the time I accidentally locked us out of the boat. I had forgotten all about it. I picked at the stitches with my nails until the seam loosened and I could ease the key out.

I looked around, suddenly worried that someone might see me, but the marina was empty. Just me, the crying gulls and the restless wind. I pushed the key into the lock, tugged it open, slid out the companionway boards, and let myself in.

Someone had stuck a rose-scented air freshener on the bulkhead, but the air in *Eliza J*'s cabin was heavy with the dank musty smell of mildew and neglect. I opened the portholes and lifted the V-berth hatch, letting the breeze blow through. I switched on the house battery and turned on the cabin lights, brightening the gloom. Through the open companionway, I could see the sky getting lighter.

If Mom was here, we'd be getting the sail covers off, opening the water intake, starting the engine, pulling out the chart book. Unless we were just sailing to Sidney Spit or something. Mom knew that route like the back of her hand. Even I could do that trip without charts.

My breath caught in my throat. I could do it. Right now. And if I was ever going to sail *Eliza J* again, this was my last chance. Quickly, before the marina office opened and people started arriving and the docks starting buzzing with the chatter and hum of a blue-sky spring Sunday.

My heart was racing. I hadn't ever sailed alone. I knew how to start the engine and raise the sails and all that, but Mom was always in charge. This was a crazy idea. Plus, if the boat was already sold, I was technically stealing it.

On the other hand, if I didn't do it, I'd never sail *Eliza J* again. I wiped my cold sweaty hands on my jeans. It was now or never.

I glanced at my watch: just past six. If I got back on my bike and went home now, Dad wouldn't even know I'd been gone. Obviously, that was what I should do.

And I might have done it, if I hadn't remembered Kathy's car in the driveway.

I lifted the valve to let fresh water cool the engine, switched over the battery and scrambled back up the companionway steps. I pushed the throttle forward slightly and touched my finger to the stiff ridged rubber of the engine start button.

I hesitated, holding my breath. Was I actually going to do this? Once I started the engine, I told myself, there was no turning back.

Sometimes starting the engine could be difficult, especially on cold mornings. It would strain and strain—*chugga, chugga, chugga*—but not turn over. I wasn't sure whether I would be relieved or disappointed if that happened now. I closed my eyes and pushed the button; the engine started, smooth as a kitten's purr.

I didn't want to sit here, waiting for nosy neighbors to arrive, but I was nervous about getting off the dock safely. Usually it was a two-person job: I would leap off the boat, untie the dock lines, help guide the boat as Mom reversed, and jump back aboard at the last possible minute. I had only docked and undocked by myself a couple of times, for practice. Mom had said docking was an important skill that I should learn.

I hoped I could remember everything she'd told me.

The dock swayed slightly under my feet as I stepped off the boat. I quickly untied the midship lines and coiled them neatly on the dock. Then I untied the bow line and stern line and held them in my hands, feeling the lines tighten instantly as the wind tried to push *Eliza J* away from the dock. The breeze was a bit stronger than I'd realized. I held on tightly to the ropes and tried to guide the boat backward, but she was drifting too fast, and I was scared that if the gap between the boat and the dock got any wider, I wouldn't be able to jump it. I tried to pull tighter on the bow line and felt the rough rope tug against my palm...

Next time, let go of the rope.

I tossed the rope onto the deck and jumped aboard.

I put the engine in reverse, straightened the tiller and quickly ran to the bow. The wind was making *Eliza J* swing to starboard before she was clear of the dock, and her anchor, sticking out over the bow, was dangerously close to the boat in the next slip. I grabbed a boat hook from the deck, leaned over the railing and gave our neighbor's boat a good hard shove.

And we were clear. I had done it.

I put the engine in forward and motored slowly away from the docks, out past the rocky gray breakwater and away from the marina. I took one last look back, half expecting to see someone standing at the end of the dock waving and yelling at me to come back. Dad, maybe. But there was no one there.

I slowed the engine and unzipped the sail covers from the main and jib, stowing the canvas in a cockpit locker. Then I shackled the halyards to the sails and raised first the main and then the jib. This was always my job, wrapping the halyard around the winch, heaving hand over hand as the white canvas fluttered its way upward noisily, while my mother watched from the helm, holding the boat into the wind until I gave her the thumbs-up.

I pushed the tiller gently to starboard, and *Eliza J*'s bow swung to port, away from the wind. The sails tightened as the wind filled them. *Eliza J* heeled over, leaning to one side as she headed away from shore.

Engine off. I caught my breath. This was our favorite moment, Mom's and mine: that moment when the diesel hum of the engine suddenly stopped and all that was left was the song of the wind and the sound of the hull gliding through the water and the deep gray-green of the ocean stretching out before us as far as we could see. *Ahhh…*Mom would give this long contented sigh and we'd both just sit there. Neither of us needed to say anything because we both knew how it was and that there was nowhere else we'd rather be.

I put my hand to my cheek and found my face suddenly wet with tears. There was no one watching, so I didn't bother wiping them away. I pictured Mom sitting across from me in the cockpit, and I let myself cry as *Eliza J* sailed on.

twenty

Eventually I ran out of tears, but not out of memories.

Out here, Mom seemed closer than she had since the day we'd heard the news about her disappearance. All those days we'd spent, the two of us, on *Eliza J*. I remembered playing Scrabble in the cockpit while we floated in a dead calm and waited for the wind to return. I remembered tinned pineapple and baked beans for dinner. I remembered seals and dolphins and, a couple of times, whales. I remembered getting caught in a storm one time when I was about ten, the banging and crashing and incredible noise of the boat, the way *Eliza J* heeled over so far that her rail was buried in the water, and the way the waves crashed over the bow and spray flew over the dodger and drenched us. I'd cowered in a corner of the cockpit, terrified.

But Mom had loved it. She'd reefed the sails, moving around on the wet tilting deck as agile and sure-footed as a cat, her wet hair whipping straight back in the wind. Finally, with the boat more level and the noise reduced to a slightly less deafening roar, she'd sat down beside me. *Fi, my darling, you have to learn to love the sea in all its moods.*

She was the one who'd given me Tania Aebi's book, *Maiden Voyage*. She'd believed I could do it. I looked out to the horizon and saw the dramatic snowy outline of Mount Baker, the sun slowly climbing higher in the blue sky, the waves of the ocean stretching out forever.

And for the first time in ages, I started to believe it again too.

*   *   *

The wind had started to pick up. I huddled in the cockpit, my hand practically frozen to the tiller and the canvas sail cover wrapped around me for extra warmth. Despite the sunshine, it was *cold* out here. The wind could suck every last bit of heat from your body. I glanced at my watch: ten thirty.

Dad must have been awake for a while—Kathy too, unless she got up early to sneak out. Dad might not know I was gone yet though. He'd probably think I was sleeping in. He often made waffles on the weekends, and any minute now he'd probably go up to my room to wake me up. I wondered what he would do when he discovered that I wasn't there.

Maybe he'd just assume I'd gone for a bike ride. That was the best-case scenario. Otherwise, he'd be freaking out. I felt a pang of guilt and pushed it away.

Surely I should be able to see Sidney Spit by now? I hadn't been plotting a course, just following the coastline, but now, with a clutch of fear in my chest, I realized that nothing looked familiar. Could I have missed it somehow? My teeth were starting to chatter from the cold, my nose was frozen, and my toes and fingers ached.

What if I'd missed it? Maybe I should turn back.

Don't panic, I told myself. I thought about the scene in *Maiden Voyage*, where Tania Aebi is heading out of New York harbor, sailing alone for the first time, and her engine dies. She'd been terrified, but she'd kept going. She hadn't given up.

Finally Sidney Spit came into view, a pale tongue of sand reaching out into the ocean. The wind dropped as we came closer and moved into the lee of the island. I couldn't wait to get anchored and warm up. Shivers ran through me in waves so intense, my whole body shook.

It was an easy place to anchor. The only thing I had to be careful of was not getting too close to shore. *Eliza J* had a five-foot draft, and the last thing I wanted to do was go aground in shallow water. I wasn't too worried: we'd anchored here dozens of times before. Half a dozen boats were snuggled in close to the beach, but there was plenty of room for mine.

I started the engine and dropped the sails, leaving them piled on the deck while I slowly motored in closer, looking for the perfect spot. *Right there.* It was as if Mom was there, giving me directions. I slipped the engine into neutral, ran up to the bow and lowered the anchor: hand over hand, nice and easy, letting the chain out a few feet at a time. The water was maybe twelve feet deep, plus the few feet from the water surface to the bow. If Mom and I were only staying for a couple of hours, we'd go for a four-to-one ratio and let out maybe sixty feet of chain. For staying overnight…

I stopped, the chain dangling from my hands.

I had no idea what came next. I hadn't thought beyond this moment.

In the end, I let out sixty feet of anchor chain. I reversed to make sure the anchor was properly set, digging itself securely into the sandy bottom. Then I turned off the engine and just sat there, teeth chattering and my whole body vibrating with each convulsive shiver.

Dad would be beside himself. He'd call Joni. He'd guess I'd gone there. When Joni said she hadn't seen me, he'd try Abby's house.

They'd all be freaking out.

Maybe the marina would call Dad and tell him the boat had been stolen.

He'd know it was me.

I felt a sickening tidal wave of guilt break over me. This would be Dad's worst nightmare. I knew that was true. And as angry as I was at him—about Kathy, about him not letting me sail, about his insistence on *moving on*—I knew I couldn't do this to him.

I took one last look around me and breathed in the peacefulness of the gray water and the white sand and the windswept bluffs glowing golden in the morning sun. Then, still shivering, I headed back up to the bow to pull up the anchor.

Time to go home.

twenty-one

By the time I was halfway back, I was starting to get scared. The wind kept building until it was blowing hard—not gale force, I didn't think, but awfully close. The sea was starting to heap up into large swells, and the wind was blowing spray off the tops of the waves and into the air. It had clouded over too. In every direction, the sea and sky were gray and threatening.

And I was so cold. My jeans, sweatshirt and thin fleece were no protection from the icy wind. *Eliza J* was heeled well over, waves rushing across her bow and spraying over the dodger. I'd already dropped the mainsail, so we were sailing with the jib alone. It wasn't very well balanced, but I was scared to go up on the foredeck without Mom to take the helm and hold us on course, and I didn't know how to set up the autohelm to steer the boat for me.

I was going to have to do something though. I should have the storm jib up, probably, instead of barreling along with the full jib. I eyed the foredeck: it was at a thirty-degree angle, and every few seconds a wave sent an icy sheet of water sluicing across it. The thought of inching across it, hanging on to the rigging with one frozen hand and trying to change sails with the other...what if I slipped? I didn't have a life jacket or a safety harness.

Jennifer wrote her own ticket. Was that what people would say about me if I didn't make it back?

The wind howled through the rigging, and a sheet of airborne spray sliced toward me right over the top of the dodger. I gasped as the icy water hit me, soaking me from head to foot and filling my sneakers before it swirled away down the cockpit drains.

I wasn't sure if it was more dangerous to try to change the foresail or to leave it up. *If in doubt, reduce sail*, Mom always said. But leaving the relative safety of the cockpit and venturing onto the heaving foredeck seemed suicidal.

And I was so cold.

Through the companionway, I could see the radio, and for a moment I considered calling for help.

But Mom had always said sailors had to be self-sufficient, that most people who called Mayday could have solved the problem themselves if they weren't so conditioned to depend on others. And besides, if I called for help, there would be no possible way to sneak the boat back in the marina and keep this trip a secret. Everyone would know that I had tried to sail alone and failed. I hated the thought.

"Mom!" I shouted. "Mom! If you are out here, please help me! Tell me what to do!" My voice was hoarse, and my teeth were chattering so hard my words sounded stiff and strange. "Mom! I need you!"

All I could hear was the wind. What was I doing out here? I pictured Dad waking up and looking for me; Joni answering the phone, morning coffee in her hand; Tom trying to be reassuring; everyone panicking when they realized the boat was gone.

I was crying now, in painful gasping sobs, and my hands were so cold I could barely hold on to the tiller. I let go, burying my hands inside my jacket to warm them. *Eliza J* turned away from the wind, her jib sail whipping across the deck and backfilling. We were drifting now, pushed along by the wind and current, no longer even pointing toward home.

"Help!" I shouted. "Someone, please help me! Please!" The wind snatched my words away and drowned them in the tumble of waves and spray.

I felt more alone and more frightened than I had ever felt in my life. The whole situation seemed unreal. A nightmare, only I knew I wasn't going to wake up.

I didn't want to die out here. I suddenly remembered Dad saying he couldn't imagine what Kathy had gone through, losing both her partner and her child: *I don't think I could survive that,* he'd said.

I wondered what my mother had felt in those last minutes or hours after her boat hit the reef: whether she had wished she hadn't gone on the trip; whether she had felt guilty about leaving me; whether she had thought she would be rescued or realized that she was going to die. Whether, like Kathy had said, she had felt regret.

And I stumbled to my feet, climbed down into the cabin and picked up the radio.

*

* *

* *

It seemed like a long time before help came. The coast guard had relayed my call, asking any boats in the area to lend assistance. *Eliza J* didn't have a GPS, and I hadn't been plotting our course, so I could only give a rough guess at where I was: halfway between Sidney and Victoria, a mile or two offshore. I huddled in the cockpit, clutching the mike and checking in with the coast guard every few minutes, and scanning the sea for another boat.

Dad was going to kill me, I thought, but I was too scared and cold to care. I just wanted to go to sleep.

"Fiona!" Someone was shouting at me. "Fiona! Ahoy, *Eliza J*!"

I struggled to sit up. A pale blue powerboat was coming up alongside: the man from the next slip at the marina.

"Can you hear me?" he shouted.

"Yes." I nodded.

"I'm going to throw you a rope. Cleat it securely at the bow. Can you do that?"

I nodded again. A few seconds later, a coil of rope landed beside me in the cockpit. I picked it up and crawled forward, inching my way up to the foredeck. I couldn't remember the man's name. Mom liked him. She used to tease him: *When are you going to get rid of that stinkpot and get a real boat?*

My hands were so numb. I fumbled with the rope, trying to wrap it around the cleat, but it kept slipping from my fingers. It was like trying to tie a knot while wearing a baseball mitt. It took me a couple of minutes, but eventually I managed to wrap the line around the cleat in a figure-eight knot. I nodded to the man on the powerboat that I'd done it.

"Go down below and call me on seventy-two," he shouted.

I dragged myself back to the cockpit, down the companionway steps and into the cabin. It felt like a long, long way, and I kept forgetting what I was supposed to do next. Sleep. I just wanted to sleep.

"*Eliza J, Eliza J.*"

I picked up the radio and fumbled for the Transmit button. "I'm here."

"I'm going to tow you in," he said. "It's not far. You almost made it back, you know."

"Okay."

"Take off your wet clothes and wrap yourself in whatever dry stuff you can find. Can you do that?"

I nodded.

"Fiona! Can you do that?"

"Yes. I can do that."

"Okay. Call me when you've done it."

I stripped off my wet things. My whole body was trembling, and my hands were so numb I could barely use them. Hypothermia, I told myself. You're hypothermic. I looked around for something to wrap myself in. When Mom and I used to sail, we had all kinds of stuff down here—blankets, sweaters, jackets, food, games and books. But now the boat was empty. Sold.

I stood there for a few seconds, naked, trying to force my frozen brain to think. Something dry. I opened the big storage locker under the port berth and pulled out the genoa sail in its big canvas bag. It was our sail for light winds: red and white striped and enormous. And dry. I dumped it onto the cabin floor and wrapped it around myself, over and over and over. I pushed *Transmit.* "Done it."

"Good girl," the man said. "Now hang in there. We'll be back before you know it."

*
· × ·
* *

I was still curled up on the cabin floor, wrapped in my sail, when *Eliza J* was towed alongside the marina gas dock. Voices were calling my name: Dad. Joni. I struggled to sit up. The boat rocked as people stepped on board.

"Fiona." Dad's face appeared in the companionway. All I could think was how odd it was to see him on the boat. I couldn't even remember the last time he'd been on board. It had been years.

"What on earth…? Where have you…? We've been beside ourselves with worry. When I woke up…" His words spilled out, all broken up.

I remembered the car in our driveway. "You and K-K-Kathy?" My teeth chattered.

He stared at me, his face flushing from white to angry red. "Is that what this is about? Kathy spending the night? Fiona, you could have been—"

Joni caught up to him and put her hand on his shoulder. When she does that, it's like she's breathing calmness right into you. I could actually see Dad sort of slow down and take a deep breath. "Fiona," he said, "this is really none of your business, but just listen to me a second. Kathy came over because she'd had a big fight with Caitlin and Caitlin ran off to spend the night at a friend's place. Kathy was upset and needed a friend."

"All night?"

He shook his head. "She'd had a few drinks. I didn't think she should drive, so she stayed. In the spare room, although that is none of your business either."

Ugh. I didn't want to think about my dad being with anyone. I didn't even want him to think I was thinking about it.

"I can't believe you took the boat out. You could have drowned. Anything could have happened. What were you thinking?" Dad's voice shook.

"Peter, that can wait. Look at her. She's shivering. Fi, honey, your lips are blue," Joni said.

Over her shoulder, the man from the powerboat appeared. "Here. Sweater and track pants. They're mine, but they'll fit you better than that sail." He dropped the clothes beside me on the floor. "And a hot-water bottle."

"Thanks." I hugged its warmth to my chest. Even through all the layers of sail, it felt so good it made me want to cry.

"Are you naked under there?" Joni asked.

"More or less," I said, embarrassed.

"Can you manage?"

I nodded, and they all stepped off the boat and waited on the dock while I fumbled my way into the clothes, which dangled from my wrists and bunched up around my ankles. Their owner was probably a foot taller than me. I could hear Dad and Joni thanking him and him saying it was no trouble, no trouble at all.

For him, maybe. Now that I was safely back at the dock, I was starting to wonder how much trouble *I* was in. Still shivering and holding the water bottle against my chest as if it was a shield, I made my way out to the cockpit to face my dad and Joni.

Dad's arms were folded, his jaw tight. "And now would you like to tell me where you've been?"

I started to cry. I couldn't help it. My words came out hiccupy and broken up, my teeth still chattering. "I sailed. To Sidney Spit."

"You sailed all the way to Sidney? By yourself? Fiona, that's…that's…"

"The sort of thing Jennifer would have done." Joni's voice was soft.

"Exactly." Dad was practically shouting. "Dangerous. Ill-considered. Impulsive." He shook his head, and a gust of wind blew his long strands of hair right off his bald patch and held them standing straight up like a sail in the wind. "Irresponsible. Completely irresponsible."

I scowled at my father. He hardly ever talked about Mom, and now he sounded like he was mad at her. "She was not irresponsible."

"If she wasn't irresponsible, she'd still be here," Dad said. "Obviously it's just as well that I sold the boat. I can't believe you'd do something so stupid. So *dangerous.*"

My tears dried up instantly, and I felt myself harden, my spine stiffening, my anger closing around me like a protective shell. "It wasn't dangerous," I said. "Anyway, if you were so worried, you should have asked Kathy. Surely she could have used her psychic powers and told you I was fine."

"Don't start," he said. "Come on, Fiona. Let's go. Kathy is waiting at home—at our place—in case you showed up there."

Kathy is waiting at home. I sat down in the cockpit. "I'm not going home if she's there."

"Don't be ridiculous, Fiona. You are in enough trouble already." Dad reached out his hand toward me. "Come on. Don't make this worse."

I wondered if Kathy was going to move in with us. I didn't think I could stand it if she did. I'd run away. I turned away from him and looked out at the water. I knew I was being childish, but I didn't care.

"I won't come," I said, still with my back turned. "I won't ever go in the house if she's there. I'd rather be dead."

There was an awful silence. *Dead, dead, dead.* I wished I could reach out and snatch the word back. I didn't mean it.

"Damn it, Fiona." Dad raised his voice. "Let's go. Now. I'm not kidding around."

What would he do if I just sat here in the cockpit and refused to get off the boat? I wrapped my arms around myself and tried to stop shivering.

"Peter." Joni spoke firmly. "I'll take Fiona to my place and get her warmed up. You go home and let Kathy know that Fiona is all right. I'm sure she's terribly worried."

Dad's voice was strained. "I just can't believe you did this, Fiona. Stealing a boat that doesn't even belong to us anymore. Running away. What were you thinking?"

Joni spoke so softly, it was almost a whisper. "Go, Peter. You can sort things out later. And Fiona didn't see it as stealing. You know that. And I don't think she was really running away."

"Jennifer never saw *her* trips as running away either." Dad's voice was as stiff and hollow as an empty hull. Gutted. Like there was space inside him that the wind could blow right through.

There was a long silence.

"Peter, I'm taking her home. She's hypothermic, and the first thing here is to get her warmed up. If you try to talk to her now, you'll both end up saying things you'll regret. She's too cold to think clearly anyway. Let me look after her for the afternoon. It'll give you both time to cool off."

Another long silence. *Warm up*, I thought vaguely. *Cool off.* I stifled a giggle. Maybe Joni was right: I wasn't thinking clearly.

"Fine," Dad said at last. "Fiona, will you go with Joni?"

I turned to face them both. Dad's face had this awful crumpled look, and I avoided meeting his eyes. I nodded quickly. "I guess so."

Dad turned and walked off down the dock without a word. I was surprised he'd actually gone: I'd half expected to be picked up and carried screaming to the car like a little kid.

Joni sighed. "Oh dear. I'm afraid your father isn't too happy with me."

"I'm not too happy with him," I said, stepping off the boat.

She shook her head. "He's been a wreck all morning. Convinced something terrible had happened. So his anger…well, that's where it's coming from."

"You must have been worried too, but you're not yelling at me."

Joni shuddered and closed her eyes for a second. When she opened them again, they were shining with tears. "You have no idea, Fiona. No idea."

I swallowed. "I'm sorry, Joni. I didn't think."

"We've all been completely terrified. I think your dad's aged about ten years." She shook her head. "Come on. My car's in the parking lot."

"I have to tidy up first. Put the sails away and all that."

Joni knocked on the hull of the powerboat, and the owner poked his head out the door. "Do you think you could take care of *Eliza J*? I want to get Fiona home and warm."

"Not a problem," he said.

"Don't forget to close the engine intake," I said. "And turn off the battery."

He winked at me. "Don't you worry."

"Thanks a lot, Mike," Joni said. "For everything." Her voice wobbled, and she started crying.

"Shock," he said gruffly. "Go on home. She'll be fine."

Joni clutched my arm as we walked to the car, her grip uncomfortably tight. Tears were streaking her cheeks, and she kept shaking her head.

"I'm really sorry I scared you," I said.

"Just get in the car." Joni opened the passenger door. "And please don't ever do anything like that again."

I stuck my hand in the pocket of the oversized sweats and felt the cool metal of *Eliza J*'s key. I wasn't sure why I had kept it, but at the last minute, I hadn't wanted to leave it behind.

We were halfway to Joni's house, the heater in her car blasting warm air at my face and feet, when something suddenly struck me. "Joni? The man on the power-boat? You called him Mike."

"What about him?"

"Is that short for Michael?"

She looked at me oddly. "I imagine so."

I started to laugh.

"You're hysterical," Joni said, shaking her head. "It's the cold."

Kathy had seen the name *Michael. He could be from your past or future*, she'd told me. And now someone called Michael had more or less saved my life. I didn't want to think about what that meant.

twenty-two

Joni's house was warm and smelled of baking, but I couldn't stop shivering. Joni loaned me two thick sweaters and made me wear them both, one on top of the other. Tom padded into the kitchen in his housecoat and made us all mugs of hot chocolate. Joni piled cookies onto a plate. When I was snuggled up on the couch with a comforter and the refilled hot-water bottle, she sat down beside me.

"How are you feeling?" she asked. "You're still shivering."

I looked at her face, lined with worry and puffy-eyed from crying, and the craziness of what I had done hit me all over again. "Joni? I was sure I could do it. I really was. But I was so cold, and it got so windy." I hugged myself, trying to stop the shaking. "I was scared. Really scared."

"You did the right thing, calling for help."

I opened my mouth to say something, but my chin was trembling, and I felt like I might start to cry again myself. "I thought I might die," I choked out. "I called Mom, you know? To tell me what to do. To help me."

"Oh, Fiona." Joni's face creased with pain.

"And she didn't answer." I sniffed and wiped my eyes on a fold of the comforter.

"No. She couldn't. She's gone, Fiona. I wish she wasn't, but—"

I cut her off. "I met Kathy before. I mean, before she knew who I was. She did a reading for me downtown, in a store. With Abby. And she said…she told me she had this vision about Mom."

All Joni said was, "Really," but her eyes hardened, and I could tell she was working hard to hold back her feelings.

"At first I thought she might be for real. I thought maybe I could talk to Mom again." A tear escaped and traced a warm line down to my upper lip. I brushed it off and tasted salt.

Joni leaned toward me. "Does your father know about this?"

I shook my head. "I didn't tell him. But it doesn't matter, because now I know for sure she's a liar.

If Mom could really communicate with anyone, she would have helped me out there today. There was no way she'd talk to Kathy but ignore me shouting for help."

"I don't know what to say, Fiona. I don't believe in any of this psychic stuff, you know that."

"It's confusing." I twisted a fold of comforter between my fingers. "I mean, I know she's lying, but then she'll get something right. Like she said someone called Michael might be important. And that guy who came and got me on his boat was called Mike."

Joni shrugged. "It's a very common name. I guess if someone makes enough predictions, sooner or later some of them will come true."

"Yeah, I suppose." Something else occurred to me. "And besides, Kathy couldn't find me, could she? Her psychic powers couldn't tell you where I was."

Joni shook her head. "She was certain you were at Abby's, actually, so I drove over there. They were just getting back from church. Abby was the one who guessed you'd be at the marina."

Ha. "That should prove it to Dad, then," I said. "That should convince him Kathy's a fake."

Joni looked horrified. "Fiona! Please tell me that isn't why you did this."

"No, I never even thought of it. But it'd be worth freezing solid if it meant Dad would forget about Kathy."

"Oh, Fiona. Do you really hate her so much?"

I squirmed. "I thought you were on my side."

"There are no sides here, honey." Joni took a careful sip from her mug. "I love you, that's all. And your dad loves you. We all want you to be happy."

Across the room, Tom sat down in his old rocking chair. "Of course we do," he said.

"How am I supposed to be happy about Dad dating a professional liar?" I asked.

Joni gave a helpless shrug and looked at Tom.

"Are you warming up?" he asked.

"My hands are tingling." I held them out to show him how red they were.

Tom winced. "Can't believe you went out there without decent clothes. Still shivering?"

"Not so much." I still couldn't imagine ever being warm again, but the shivers that had been shaking my whole body seemed to have subsided at last.

"Hungry?"

I realized I was. "Starving."

He grinned at me and got to his feet. "Scrambled eggs special deluxe, made by your talented and terribly handsome personal chef?"

I looked at Tom standing there in his ratty house-coat, with his round belly and his hair sticking up in all directions, and I had to laugh. "Yes, please," I said. Dragging the comforter along with me, I followed him into the kitchen.

twenty-three

Tom cracked two eggs into a silver bowl and whisked them with a fork: *clickety-clickety-click*. He cleared his throat. "Listen, chickie. This business about you hating Kathy. You know what happened, right? To her older daughter and her husband?"

I narrowed my eyes, hoping he wasn't going to try to make me feel sorry for her. "She told me. But that doesn't make it okay for her to lie."

Tom rinsed a mushroom under the tap, put it on a wooden chopping board and started slicing it. "I just wondered if it might make a difference if you could see her as someone who has found a way of coping with a terrible loss." He looked at me and raised his eyebrows. "Someone who needed to believe something a little unusual to make her reality more bearable."

Joni sat down on the stool beside mine. "I think Tom's right, Fiona. Your dad told me that Kathy is absolutely convinced that she can communicate with people who've died."

"Poor Caitlin," Tom said.

I'd expected him to say *poor Kathy*. "Losing her dad and her sister, you mean?"

"Well, that must have been an awful thing to go through, of course. Unimaginably awful." Tom opened the fridge door and stuck his head halfway inside, still talking. "But on top of that, now she has to grow up in the shadow of a perfect older sister. A ghost sister that her mom talks to all the time." He pulled his head out and made a face. "You've got to wonder what that's like."

I hadn't thought much about any of this from Caitlin's point of view. Dad had tried to point out that Caitlin had her own grief to deal with, but I hadn't wanted to hear it. "I haven't been very nice to Caitlin," I confessed.

"Not too late to start." Tom plonked a block of cheddar on the counter and sliced off a few thin ribbons of cheese. "You can't go too far wrong by being kind."

I wondered how I'd cope if Dad pretended that he could still talk with Mom. It seemed to me that Caitlin was one more reason Kathy shouldn't make up things that weren't true. How was she supposed to deal with losing her dad and sister if her own mother pretended they weren't really gone?

"Even if Kathy does believe it all, she's still a liar," I said. "She's lying to herself."

"Oh, we all lie to ourselves." Joni put her mug down and leaned closer to me. "I think you might be lying to yourself a little bit if you think your anger is just about Kathy."

"What do you mean?"

"Look how angry your dad was today. Do you think that was all about what you did?"

Her words didn't make sense to me. I felt like my brain was full of fog. "What else would it be about?"

Joni's voice was slow, patient. "Well, he seemed pretty angry with your mom too. Don't you think? People often feel angry when someone dies. Angry that the person isn't around anymore. Angry that they have to keep going without them."

I nodded, but the fog inside my brain felt thicker than ever. So thick, I could barely hear what she was saying, let alone make sense of it.

"Maybe you're a bit angry about that too," Joni said.

"It isn't fair for us to be mad at Mom. She didn't mean to die!" But in the back of my mind, all the things I'd been trying not to think were getting louder and more insistent. Dad yelling at her:

The least you can do is take along the technology to communicate. A satellite phone, maybe. And the conversation I overheard at the marina. That self-righteous woman shaking her head, saying, *Jennifer wrote her own ticket.*

"No. But we aren't always rational in how we feel."

I watched Tom pour the eggs into the hot pan. My eyes started to prickle, and I pulled the comforter more tightly around my shoulders. "Dad wanted her to take more precautions," I whispered. "Safety equipment, stuff like that. So that rescue boats could find her if there was a problem. And I took her side. I said he didn't know anything about sailing."

"Well, he doesn't." Joni studied my face. "Honey, you aren't blaming yourself, are you?"

I blinked back tears. "I don't know. Sort of."

"Well, don't. Your mother was an adult and an experienced sailor. She made her own decisions." Joni shook her head. "Besides, she had flares and a life raft. It wasn't that rescuers couldn't find her. People reported the location of the flares. It was just that it was so rough, and they were so far from anywhere. By the time people could respond, it was too late."

I nodded. "If I'd asked her not to go…"

"You really think she'd have listened?" Joni raised her eyebrows.

"Your father asked her not to go plenty of times," Tom reminded me. He scraped the mess of eggs off the bottom of the pan with a plastic spatula, flipping it over like a pancake. "Jennifer always did what she wanted to do."

"I know. I just miss her, that's all." I felt empty and tired. "And I can't stand that no one talks about her anymore. Dad doesn't. Even you don't, Joni."

"Oh, honey. I suppose we all worry about you. We don't want to upset you." She looked at Tom. "Right?"

He cleared his throat. "Right."

"I don't want to forget her," I whispered.

"You won't forget her," Joni said.

I didn't say anything for a minute. My head was full of words, but I couldn't speak. Mostly what I was thinking was that she was wrong. When I was on *Eliza J*, Mom seemed close, but the rest of the time, she didn't. I was already forgetting stuff. It was getting harder and harder to picture her face, and even though it had only been a year, my memories of her were starting to get that stories-and-snapshots feeling—shrinking, and becoming sort of disconnected and distant. Sometimes I thought it was because I conjured them up too often, playing and replaying scenes in my head. I wondered if a memory could get worn out.

"Voilà," Tom said, sliding a steaming plate of eggs in front of me. "Scrambled eggs special deluxe."

I stared down at the eggs for a few seconds and watched them blur.

"Fiona? What are you thinking?" Joni tilted her head, trying to see my face.

"I'm scared I'll forget." I looked at Joni through the haze of tears. "Not completely. You know. Just, like, some things."

She balanced her mug on the giant stack of magazines on the kitchen counter. "I want to show you something. Just a minute, okay?" She left the room, throwing an anxious glance back over her shoulder. "Eat those eggs, okay?"

"Eat up," Tom agreed. "Come on. Get something warm inside you."

I took a bite of hot cheesy eggs. And another and another. I was starving. I'd wolfed down the whole plateful by the time Joni came back.

She put a photo album down in front of me on the kitchen counter. "It's something I've been putting together. Just for myself, I guess, though I imagined I'd give it to you someday."

I stared at the album. Dark blue cover with a cutaway circle in the center and my mom's face looking out at me. An old photo, one from before

I was born, with Mom looking right at the camera, smiling, or maybe even laughing, mouth slightly open, chin lifted and head tilted back in that way she had. I ran my fingers lightly across the dark blue cover.

"You can…" Joni gestured at the book. "If you want to look at it."

I nodded and opened the cover, expecting to see another picture. Instead, I saw Joni's big loopy handwriting.

To Jennifer, who will always be my Little Sister.

I remember you coming home from the hospital, so much smaller than I expected. Mom let me choose your middle name: Michelle, after the Beatles' song. I used to dance around the house with you in my arms, singing it to you. I remember helping you learn to walk: holding your hands around and around the kitchen table, you insisting on more, more, more, and screaming in frustration as your white socks slipped on the linoleum. I was sixteen; you were just past your first birthday, but even as a baby, you were determined to do things your own way.

I swallowed hard. "You wrote that?" I flipped ahead. Pages and pages…

Joni's face was several shades pinker than usual. "I know it isn't brilliant writing, but it wasn't meant for people to read. It's a memory book."

"Wow. This is all about Mom?"

"My little sister," Joni said. "I can't believe how much I miss her. Every day." Her eyes were wet, the wrinkles around them shining with tears, but she smiled at me. "I won't forget her, you know."

I realized that I hadn't actually thought that much about what Mom's death had meant to Joni. She'd always been there for me to lean on, but she must have felt almost as bad as I did. "She was amazing, wasn't she?" I said.

"The best."

Tom cleared his throat again. "Look, I've been sitting over here telling myself to stay out of this, to mind my own business."

"Sounds like good advice," Joni said, her voice suddenly sharp. "Maybe you should take it."

I looked at him curiously. Tom doesn't speak seriously all that often, and he hates conflict, but Joni sounded almost angry. She sounded as if she knew what he was going to say before he even said it.

Tom dropped the frying pan into the sink and turned to face us. He pointed at Joni's memory book. "It's just…oh, come on, Joni. I know you loved her, but Jennifer drove you crazy when she was alive. You're saying you don't want to forget her, but honestly? Sometimes I think you already have."

I listened, torn between wanting to put my hands over my ears—*la la la la I can't hear you*—and wanting him to say more. To talk about Mom and make her feel real again.

Joni stood up. "Tom. Stop it."

He turned toward me. "I loved your mom. You know that, right?"

I nodded.

"Jennifer was probably the most energetic, fun, passionate person I have ever met. You know how people talk about trying to live in the moment? Well, she did that. Life was one long series of great moments for her." He shrugged. "And she was also one of the most selfish, stubborn people I've known."

"Tom! How can you say that?" Joni's face flushed an angry mottled red, and she glared at him furiously.

He glared right back. "I don't think you're doing Fiona any favors by putting Jennifer on a pedestal. You know what she was like."

There was a long silence. Finally Tom turned away from Joni and looked at me. "I don't mean to upset you," he said. "I loved your mom. But you know what? She wasn't perfect."

I couldn't force a single word past the lump in my throat, but I nodded to let him know it was okay. I understood. Maybe I should be angry like Joni was, but it was weird: what I felt was more like relief. We'd been reducing Mom to a cardboard cutout of herself. And Mom was anything but a cardboard cutout. "I know," I managed at last. "She could be pretty set on getting what she wanted."

Joni slammed her memory book shut and looked at me like I was the worst kind of traitor. Shaking her head, she stalked out of the room, clutching the book to her chest.

"Don't worry," Tom said. "It's me she's mad at, not you. She'll get over it."

I watched the empty doorway. I couldn't remember Joni ever walking out on me before. "I overheard Dad say something one time, before Mom left. He said he'd had enough." I looked up at Tom. "Do you think that they were going to get divorced?"

Tom shook his head. "People say things when they're upset."

"They fought a lot."

"Like cats and dogs. But they stayed together, didn't they? Anyway, there's not much point in speculating. I'd put that thought right out of your head, if you can."

"Okay." Obviously Tom couldn't know for sure, but his words still made me feel better. I wanted to believe that my parents would have worked it out.

"Truth is," he said, "Jennifer was the baby of the family and spoiled rotten by her parents and by Joni. She was a bit too used to getting her own way. Used to drive Joni crazy sometimes."

I remembered Mom shouting at my dad: *All I'm trying to do is live my life the way I want to. To follow my dreams.* I bit my lip. "Tom? Isn't it a good thing to try to live the way you want? To not let anyone get in the way of your dreams?"

Tom scratched his chest. "Well, I'm not saying it's a bad thing, chickie. But it doesn't hurt to pay a little attention to how your choices affect everyone else. Try putting yourself in their shoes once in a while. No man is an island, and all that."

"Mom did think about other people," I said stubbornly. I knew he was right. Mom had thought about me, though maybe not always very clearly. But she didn't think about Dad.

"She loved you," Tom said. His eyes were shining and pink-rimmed. "And I miss her too, Fiona. I miss having you and her and Peter over here, playing games and laughing and eating too much. I miss Jennifer's laugh. I miss arguing with her. I even miss her stupid stubborn pride."

I swallowed. "Me too. Tom?"

"Yeah?"

"I'm going to talk to Joni, okay? Make sure she's okay."

He nodded. "You do that, chickie."

*   *   *

Joni was sitting on the edge of her bed, crying. She looked up when I walked in.

"Joni? Are you okay?"

"Just sad," she said, wiping her eyes. "Which is okay, right?"

I nodded. "Please don't be mad at Tom."

"Oh, he can be such an idiot sometimes. No sense of timing."

"I don't want you guys to fight."

"Don't worry. It wouldn't be the first time." She gave me a halfhearted smile. "I'll get over it. Sorry I stomped off. I'm just not ready to hear him talk about Jennifer like that." She tilted her head, studying my face. "Has he upset you? He can be so insensitive sometimes."

"No. Not really." I sat down beside her. "It sort of helped, in a way. There's this way everyone talks about people after they're dead, like they're suddenly perfect. And it was kind of nice to have someone not do that.

It made Mom seem less far away, somehow." I looked up at her anxiously. "Sometimes I even have trouble picturing her face, you know?"

"Ahh. Yes, I do know." Joni stood up, walked over to her bookshelf and pulled something off a pile. "I have something for you. If you want it."

She handed me a book. Big, square, dark blue. A square picture in the center: a tiny sailboat with ocean all around it.

I opened the cover. Blank pages.

"I thought perhaps you could make your own memory book. Writing, photos, whatever you want." Joni sat back down beside me. "I bought it ages ago, but I wasn't sure…"

"I love it." I already knew what was going on the first page: a picture of me and Mom together on *Eliza J.* It's not a great picture; Mom took it, holding the camera out in front of us, too close and not very straight. But we're both laughing, and the wind is blowing our hair across our faces. I remembered that moment so clearly. It was one of those perfect sailing days. "I wish Dad hadn't sold *Eliza J,*" I whispered.

"I know." Joni patted my knee. "You know, I don't mean to sound like I don't see how hard that is—but there will be other boats. If you really want to sail, you'll make it happen. You're like your mom that way—determined. But *Eliza J* wasn't the only boat your Mom loved, and she won't be the only one for you either."

"Dad won't even let me sail," I reminded her.

"Give it time," Joni said. "Give it time."

twenty-four

Joni called ahead first to check whether Kathy was there.

"You have to go home either way," she told me. "But you might as well feel prepared."

When she told me that Kathy was spending the evening at home with Caitlin, I felt relieved for about a second before I started getting anxious about being alone with Dad. I knew he'd be expecting me to apologize for worrying him, and I guess for technically stealing the boat. It hadn't felt like stealing—*Eliza J* was mine, no matter what it said on paper. Of course, I knew I shouldn't have taken off in the boat, but I was too mad about Dad selling *Eliza J* to tell him that I was sorry.

Anyway, I *wasn't* entirely sorry. I felt bad about scaring everyone, but in a way I was glad I'd done it.

Glad, glad, glad. Even if it was dangerous, even if it was selfish and irresponsible, even though I'd needed help to get home. In some crazy way, it had been exactly what I needed to do. Every time I thought about being out there alone, just me and *Eliza J* skimming across the waves on our way to Sidney Spit, I felt a flutter of excitement and beneath that, a steady warmth. Someday I would sail around the world. Even if Dad wouldn't let me sail now, at least I had my dream back again. No one could take that away.

Joni drove me home, and to my surprise, she gave me a big hug goodbye, crushing me against her cushiony warmth. I held on tightly for a few seconds before letting go. "Thanks, Joni."

"Love you, kiddo." Her voice was gruff.

"Love you too."

"Now get in there. It'll all work itself out, don't you worry." She looked me in the eyes. "He loved your mom, you know, despite their differences. And he loves you too."

I nodded and blinked away tears. Then I got out of her car and headed inside.

Dad was in the kitchen making dinner. Pizza. It was something Mom used to make pretty often, but I couldn't remember Dad ever making it before. We usually ordered in or went to Paul's Pizza Palace. I leaned against the counter and watched as he sprinkled cheese over the other toppings.

"The pepperoni goes crispier if you put it on top of the cheese," I told him.

"Am I making this pizza, or are you?"

"Sorry. Just trying to help." The pizza had made me hopeful that he wasn't too angry, but apparently he was. I hadn't ever done anything as bad as stealing a boat before. Nothing even close. I wondered what Dad was going to do to me. Ground me, maybe. I'd never been grounded before. Dad had always been stricter than Mom, but she had made most of the decisions when it came to me, and she always argued that parenting shouldn't be about coercion. *We can't expect kids to grow up with their own sense of values if we just demand certain behavior*, she said to Abby's mom one time. Abby told me her mother thought my mom was way out there, but that she liked her a lot anyway. You couldn't help liking someone who smiled as much as my mom did.

Dad had the pizza stone heated up in the oven, and he was getting ready to slide the raw pizza onto it. He'd stretched the crust super thin and loaded it with toppings. I had a bad feeling as he started to lift it.

I opened my mouth to say something and snapped it closed again. His pizza, not mine.

The pizza folded, tore and collapsed in a sloppy mess on the hot stone.

Dad swore under his breath.

"It might be okay," I said. "If we straighten it out…"

He put on the oven mitts, picked up the pizza stone and dumped the whole thing in the garbage. "I don't think so."

I don't know why, but I started crying. Out of the blue. One minute I was just standing there, and the next I was crying, crying, crying. I felt like I might never stop.

"Honey…" Dad stared at me, his oven-mitted hands hanging at his sides. "It's just a *pizza*."

I shook my head and gasped noisily, trying to catch my breath. It wasn't just the pizza that was a mess. It was everything. It was me and Dad, trying to muddle on without Mom. I wasn't sure that we would be able to straighten it out at all.

"Look." He sighed. "Can you…could you please stop crying? We have to talk."

I took a few more shuddering gasps, nodding and trying to stop. "Mom always used cornmeal," I whispered.

"What?"

"Cornmeal. Under the pizza. To make it slide more easily." I wiped my eyes with my sleeve and sniffed. "She said it worked like tiny ball bearings."

"Huh." Dad shook his head. "How'd you feel about ordering takeout?"

"I don't care."

"Toast and beans?"

"Fine." I wasn't hungry. "Dad, I'm sorry you were worried. I didn't mean to scare you."

"Didn't you?" He looked at me thoughtfully.

"I didn't! Honest. I didn't even think about that part." I sat down, elbows on the kitchen table, and rested my chin on my folded hands. "I didn't even mean to go. I just went to see *Eliza J* because…just because. But when I saw the Sold sign, I needed to sail her again. One last time." I wanted him to understand. "I guess I had to say goodbye."

Dad came and sat down across from me. His eyes were red and puffy, and I wondered if he'd been crying.

I had only seen my father cry twice. The first time was when I was eight and my grandma—his mom— died. He'd cried at her funeral. I remembered looking up at him and seeing his cheeks streaked with tears and feeling like I was standing on an elevator that was going down really fast.

Dad didn't cry when we heard that the boat Mom was crewing on had been found, all broken up on the reef, but when the life raft was discovered floating empty, he'd sat down on my bed. "I don't think we should hold out hope any longer," he'd said. And then, finally, he'd cried.

Up until that day, during those weeks when Mom was missing, I hadn't been too worried. I'd been sure she would show up sooner or later. It was Dad crying that convinced me that she wouldn't ever be coming home.

"Dad." I hoped I wasn't going to start crying again. "I am really, really sorry I scared you."

He shook his head and didn't answer right away. I wondered if he was thinking of Mom. *Safer at sea in a good boat than out on the highway in a car.* That's what she always said.

"It was a stupid thing to do, Fiona. Dangerous and stupid and unbelievably inconsiderate. You could have fallen overboard, you could have drowned, you... do you even have any idea what you put us all through?" His voice shook slightly.

"I didn't think," I said. "It just sort of happened."

"I've been trying all afternoon to figure out what to say to you. To make you understand." He ran his fingers through his hair. "But honestly, I'm not sure that there is much more to say about it."

"Are you going to ground me? Or something?"

"Do you think that would be helpful?"

"No. But you said we had to talk, so…" I looked up at him. "What did you want to talk about then?"

"Kathy." He reached across the table and put his hands over mine. "Kathy and me."

My heart thudded. "You aren't…she isn't going to move in here? Is she?"

Dad looked startled. "No. We're nowhere near that kind of a decision. I'm not even sure we ever will be."

"You're not?"

"Honey, it hasn't been that long. We're just getting to know each other."

I frowned. "So why all the business about me and her needing to get to know each other? Why force Caitlin and me to hang out?"

"Well…" He raked his fingers through his hair. "That was a mistake, perhaps. I wanted you to feel included, I suppose. I didn't want you to think that me seeing someone would mean I wasn't going to be there for you."

"I didn't *want* to be included. I still don't. Kathy and Caitlin aren't family."

"No," Dad agreed. "Not now. Maybe not ever. But who knows what the future holds?"

"Not Kathy," I said.

"Fiona." Dad banged a fist on the table. "*This* is what I want to talk about. The constant smart remarks. The rudeness."

I opened my mouth to object, but he kept talking. "I am quite aware that no one will ever replace your mother. Okay? No one will ever take her place for me either." He looked down at his hands and touched the gold band he wore on his ring finger. "But life has to go on. I am going to be spending time with Kathy, and I'd like you to treat both of us with respect."

"Sorry," I said. "I just…don't get mad again, but doesn't it bother you? The psychic thing? That she believes stuff that isn't…can't…be true?"

He shook his head. "What about you and Abby? You believe different things."

"Like what?"

"She's a Christian, right? She believes in Jesus and goes to church and all that. And to that Christian camp every summer."

Abby had gone to summer camp for as long as I'd known her, but all the stories she told me were about which boy she had a crush on, or how late the girls in her cabin stayed up talking, or—most often—what they ate. "I guess. We never talk about that stuff."

"Well, you and Kathy don't have to discuss her beliefs either."

It felt different to me, but I couldn't explain why.

Dad answered as if I had spoken aloud. "The only difference is that Kathy's beliefs are more unusual.

That's it. The only difference. Spiritualism is a religion, you know. It may not be the most conventional belief system, but it's been around for an awfully long time."

Maybe he was right. Either way, there wasn't much I could do about it.

"Fiona?"

"Yeah?"

"Do you think we have cornmeal? Maybe I should try again."

My stomach grumbled. Maybe I was hungry after all. "Probably," I said, pushing my chair back and getting to my feet. "I'll help you look."

twenty-five

Abby was still angry when I saw her at school on Monday. She gave me a narrow-eyed glare, dropped her backpack in her locker and slammed the door shut. I stood there, waiting.

"What?" she said.

"I'm sorry," I said quickly. "I am so sorry, Abby."

She wasn't going to let me off that easily. "About what, exactly?"

"Everything. I've been a jerk."

"Yeah." She looked at me. "You have."

"I'm sorry about what I said at the fair. And that I didn't tell you about Nicole. I know I should have. I mean…I just…"

"Didn't want me feeling bad for Kathy," Abby said. "I know."

I shook my head. "Stop reading my mind," I told her, taken aback but half laughing.

She shrugged. "It was kind of obvious."

"Only to you," I said. Someday Abby would be a great psychologist. I didn't doubt it for a second. "Are you still mad?"

She didn't answer right away. I bit my lip anxiously. "Abby, I know I've been awful. I've just felt so rotten inside and it kept sort of oozing out."

"Yeah, I noticed." She sighed. "Saturday night, after the psychic fair, I was so mad at you. I was imagining all these things I wanted to say to you, about how self-centered you were being and how I'd had enough of it. But yesterday when we got back from church and Joni was in our driveway freaking out because you were missing…" She shook her head. "Don't do anything like that again, okay? I was really worried."

"That I'd drown?"

"No, stupid. Well, maybe a bit, but I know you can sail. Mostly I was worried you'd be grounded for life." She punched my arm lightly. "Then I'd be stuck hanging out with people who aren't you. And that would suck. I mean, total tedium."

Life at home seemed to settle a little over the next couple of weeks. Nothing dramatic: Kathy still visited, Caitlin still hung around, and Dad and I still argued. It felt a bit better though. It was sort of like the way the waves gradually subside after a storm: you can't see them getting smaller, but after a while you notice that the wind has dropped and the motion has changed and the boat isn't getting tossed around like it was before. You realize you don't feel sick anymore and that you might even be hungry.

I started writing in my memory book. Little things mostly, but dozens of them. Pages and pages. Things Mom said to me, times we spent together. Special things. Ordinary things. Things I wanted to remember. Sometimes writing made me feel sad, but mostly it felt like I finally had somewhere safe to put all those thoughts and memories and feelings, and somehow that helped.

Finally it was the day of the science fair. Dad drove Abby and me to school so we could get our display set up in the gym before our first class.

Abby bounced up and down on her toes. "Our project is *awesome*," she said. "It looks way better than anyone else's."

I looked around the room. Dozens of tables were set up in rows, and half of them were covered with displays in various stages of completion. "You're always so competitive," I said.

"No, I'm not. I just like to have the best one, that's all." Abby was putting the finishing touch on our project, sprinkling little gold stars on the black cloth that covered our table. She stepped back from it, studying it for a moment before looking up at me, laughing. "Okay, I guess that could be called competitive. But it's not like I don't want other people to do well."

"Generous of you." A girl a couple of tables over from us was trying to balance three huge sheets of impossibly flimsy blue cardboard on her table, and I tossed her a roll of duct tape. Our own display was made from three sturdy sheets of plywood: I'd even used Mom's tools to screw proper hinges onto the boards. Abby had covered the bare wood with black paper, and our research was presented in neatly typed sheets and graphs. Across the top of the display, green and purple letters read: *PSYCHIC PHENOMENA: FACT OR FICTION?*

Except for the title, it almost looked like something from the psychic fair.

I shoved my hands in my pocket and touched metal. The key to *Eliza J*'s padlock. I wasn't planning on taking off on the boat again, but I kept it with me all the time. Just in case.

*   *   *

Mrs. Moskin came by and asked us a bunch of questions about our research and our experiments. Abby answered most of them better than I did, but I didn't do too badly.

"So one last question. Just out of curiosity, not for marks." The Mouse looked right at me, her small eyes bright. "I see from reading your conclusion that your research and experiments supported your hypothesis that psychic phenomena do not exist. Was that what you were hoping to find? Or were you hoping to be surprised?"

I had set out to prove Kathy wrong; to show she was a fraud. But more than anything, I'd wanted to believe that I could someday talk to my mom again. "Both," I said at last. "A little bit of both."

Mrs. Moskin nodded, and her voice was warm. "Thank you, Fiona. I've always felt rather that way about it myself." She smiled and walked off.

"Well," Abby said, "if I was psychic, I'd predict an A in our immediate future."

"Kathy already predicted that, remember?"

"Ha ha." Abby grinned at me. "So how are things going with her?"

I made a face. "She's okay, I guess, but I'd still rather she wasn't around."

"Is she around a lot?"

"Mmm. Yeah. But she and Dad have been doing their own thing more. They're not dragging me and Caitlin into it as much, so that's something."

"Caitlin is going to have some serious issues. I hope Kathy's putting some money aside for therapy for her. Imagine having a mom who talked to your dead sister all the time."

Even though I didn't think Kathy's conversations with Nicole were real, there was a part of me that envied her. Sometimes I thought if I could just talk to Mom for five minutes, maybe she could tell me how to cope without her. "Caitlin's not so bad, actually," I admitted. "We've started talking a bit. She's smarter than she looks."

Abby gave an exaggerated gasp of shock. "Wait a minute. Did I hear that right? Are you sticking up for Caitlin?"

"Cut it out, Abby. I'm just saying..."

"I know. I'm just giving you a hard time. So does Caitlin believe the same stuff as her mom?"

"I guess so. She sort of has to, doesn't she? For now, anyway." I looked at Abby. "What about you? Do you believe it?"

Abby shrugged. "At first I was kind of convinced by what Kathy said about Gran, but the more I thought about it, the less convinced I was. So now I don't know. I guess I mostly don't believe it, but I don't completely disbelieve it either. It's like—what did you say Tom and your dad were? Agnostic?"

"Yeah." That reminded me of something. "Hey, you know what Dad said?"

"What?"

"He said that Kathy being psychic was the same as you being Christian."

"Um, hardly!" Abby looked startled. "Tell me you're kidding."

"No, no." I rushed to explain. "Not that you and Kathy believe the same things. I think his point was more that you and I don't share the same religious views but we get along fine. So in his mind, I should be able to accept Kathy's beliefs and get along with her too."

She shrugged. "Well, I'm not that religious."

"But you go to that Christian camp and you go to church every week."

"Duh. My parents would flip if I didn't. Anyway, camp's fun." She looked thoughtful. "It's true though. I guess I do believe in God, and you don't."

"And it doesn't matter."

"No," Abby agreed. "It doesn't matter." She grinned at me. "You're stuck with me, Fiona. Sorry about that."

I grinned back. "I have to put up with you. You're the best therapist I've ever had."

"Aren't I the only one?"

"Uh, yeah. That explains it," I said, and Abby elbowed me in the ribs. Hard.

A few minutes later, the Mouse was back with a piece of paper in her hand. "Congratulations, you two," she said. "Very well done indeed." She handed us the paper. *Good work,* it read. *A thoughtful exploration of an interesting question. Nicely presented, but remember to reference your sources properly.* And beneath that: a big red B+.

Abby scowled, but I couldn't help it: I burst out laughing.

*   *   *

After school I rode my bike down to the marina. I hadn't been there since Sunday. Dad hadn't exactly forbidden me to go there and I hadn't asked. Mostly I hadn't asked because I was pretty sure he'd say no.

I coasted down the long slope toward the marina and waited for the first glimpse of masts and water. *There.* My heart lifted. The sky was a soft gray, and there was almost no wind at all. It was warm and damp, and the air felt heavy, as if it was just waiting to rain. I turned into the parking lot and jumped off at the bike racks.

A few people nodded to me as I walked along the dock, and I wondered if they'd heard about what I did. Mom always used to say that this marina was worse than a high school for gossip. I nodded back and hurried past them toward E-dock.

But *Eliza J* was gone.

There was another boat in our slip—a narrow-beamed, dark-hulled sailboat—and *Eliza J* was gone.

I walked to the end of the dock and stared out toward the horizon. Mount Baker was hidden in clouds, and the water was the same color as the sky. I fingered the key in my pocket, wondering who had bought *Eliza J* and what they were like. I wondered where she'd be sailing this summer and all the summers after this. It was so strange to think of *Eliza J* having adventures without Mom and me.

I thought about what Joni had said: *There will be other boats.* I knew it was true, but no other boat would take the place of *Eliza J*. I took the key out of my pocket and rubbed my fingers over it until the metal was warm in my hand. Then I lifted my arm and threw the key as hard as I could, in a great soaring arc over the water. It disappeared without a sound.

"Goodbye," I whispered.

I stood there for a long time, just watching the water and the misty gray horizon.

Someday I would sail again. Someday I would sail all the way around the world. I didn't know when, and I didn't know how, and I didn't know if Dad would ever be able to accept it, but I knew one thing for sure: the sea would wait for me.

acknowledgments

Over the last three years, many of my good friends have read various drafts of this novel and given me thoughtful feedback. My endlessly supportive family has provided encouragement, insight and the gift of time to write. And my fabulous editor, Sarah Harvey, worked her magic and improved the novel tremendously. I am very grateful to all of you. I would also like to thank the British Columbia Arts Council for their generous support during the writing of this novel.

ROBIN STEVENSON is the author of nine novels for children and teens, including *Impossible Things* and *A Thousand Shades of Blue*. She lives in Victoria and spends most of her time writing, reading, playing games with her six-year-old son and scheming about ways to spend more time in hotter, sunnier places. Visit her website at www.robinstevenson.com.